HARDWARE

by

James L. Hankins

HARDWARE

For information, contact James L. Hankins via e-mail at jameshankins@ocdw.com.

Cover design Copyright © 2010 by Leslie Jordan Hankins

This book is a work of fiction. Although the story is set in a real city, Gulfport, Mississippi, and some real places are mentioned, the characters and events depicted in this book are entirely fictitious and are the product of the imagination of the author. Any resemblance to actual events or persons (living or deceased) is entirely coincidental.

ISBN 978-0-615-35197-1

I hate mankind, for I think myself one of the best of them, and I know how bad I am.

–Joseph Baretti, *quoted in Boswell's Life of Samuel Johnson*

Probably the toughest time in anyone's life is when you have to murder a loved one because they're the devil.

–Emo Philips

PART I
LANCE LIVIN' LARGE

CHAPTER ONE

As he viewed the police crime scene photographs for the first time in several years, Dr. Williams marveled at the fact that they were still as vivid and disturbing as he remembered. He had never been able to completely forget the images. As he shuffled them in his hands, he regretted looking at them again.

Some things were best kept in the dark.

There were sixteen of them, large eight-by-tens in full color stuffed in an evidence envelope labeled CONFIDENTIAL in large red block letters. His set also had the word COPY stamped on the back of each photograph.

The originals, of course, were in the custody of the police.

Dr. Williams held one of the images as he leaned back in his chair, holding it up in the air to study it. They were all bad, but this one…this one had stayed with him over the years. It was an image he could never get out of his mind. Although during his years as a psychiatrist he had treated many criminally insane patients, he was not accustomed to seeing such violence in graphic, unflinching detail.

In passing, he thought of his old high school football coach, standing in front of the large blank screen in the football shack like he did every Monday afternoon, just before they watched the film of the game the Friday before. For good or ill, the action was caught on film, and coach would always smile and nod at the assembled players, knowing that whatever had been missed in the heat of real-time would always show up on the game film. Coach would yell at everyone to quiet down, then walk back to the projector, his voice booming as he did so.

"The eye in the sky doesn't lie, men. The eye in the sky doesn't lie!"

It doesn't blink, either, thought Dr. Williams, puzzling over what was so haunting about the image he held in his hands. But he knew. It was her eyes.

They were open. Even after what had happened to her, she had died with her eyes open.

The police photographer, in an effort to simply record the crime scene–the scene of the *homicide* to be more precise–had somehow managed to capture an image in time in the same way that an art photographer might have done so. Dr. Williams was certain that the police photographer had not intended such a result, but he or she had nevertheless produced a vivid and haunting work of art, the stark aftermath of a moment of madness which had claimed the life of a young woman named Amy Holmes. The photograph revealed simultaneously the horror of her death and the beauty she had once had in life.

Dr. Williams studied the image for a moment longer before placing it with the others and returning them to the envelope on his desk. He placed the envelope inside the larger, expandable file that had grown over the years to include nearly six hundred pages of legal documents and medical reports. He slid the file to the corner of his desk, an unconscious gesture to distance himself physically and emotionally from its contents. He leaned back in his chair again, lifted his arms, and ran his fingers through his hair, lacing them behind his head as he stared out his office window. The sky had been overcast since he had arrived at the office and the rain had come while he was looking at the file. He watched the rain drops spatter on his office window for a few moments and then let out a sigh. He was tired of thinking of death. It was bad enough that he was forced to deal with the murder of Amy Holmes on this dreary morning, but on top of that he had to attend a funeral at noon.

Dr. Williams glanced at the tie on his desk. He had not worn a suit in a long time. He hoped he remembered how to correctly knot the tie. He picked it up and decided to try it before his new intern arrived at the office.

The intern was to fill in while Dr. Williams attended the funeral. Dr. Williams had to prepare him on how to deal with the patient. The patient's name was Walter Eisenbeis.

He was the man who had murdered Amy Holmes.

The office where Dr. David Williams practiced the sometimes dark art of psychiatry was nestled off highway 90, along the Mississippi gulf coast, just within the Gulfport city limits. It was almost hidden behind a stand of moss-laden oak trees and most drivers–either tourists in town looking to spend time at the beach when the gambling budget was lost or locals on the way to work–did not notice it as they looked out into the calm gulf coast waters. The building itself was a modern concoction of steel and glass with only a sign that read *Psychiatry Associates* stenciled in plain white letters across the front window to give any indication as to what went on inside.

The obscured location was by design. It served the main function of the building well, which was to keep the clientele appropriately buffered from the public when, as harmless idiosyncrasies bloomed into full-blown psychoses, a visit to the psychiatrist was required. Dr. Williams had always remembered the line from the television show *Taxi*, when Alex and the rest of the cabbies had pondered over Latka's sanity as his bouts of being the suave Vic Ferrari became more frequent. Dr. Williams could not remember it word for word, but he recalled Alex's deadpan delivery with a shrug, "If you have a problem with your car, you go see a mechanic. If you have primary and secondary personality diffusion, you go see a psychiatrist."

Dr. Williams had always wanted to get the quote on a poster and hang it somewhere in the office, but it somehow did not seem appropriate, so he never did.

The old money clients came to see Dr. Williams because *he* was a member of the old money club himself. Some of them were, as Dr. Williams liked to say to his colleagues, crazy as shit-house rats. But crazy or not, they were keen on keeping a low profile, and Dr. Williams made it a point to accommodate them.

During the early stages of planning for the new office building, the architect asked Dr. Williams what he had in mind as a "concept" for the structure. Dr. Williams replied with one word.

Discretion.

That is precisely what he got.

As it began to rain, the beginning of a nasty gulf coast storm, Helen Wilhoit sat behind the reception desk trying to adjust her chair. Helen was the only secretary at *Psychiatry Associates*, in fact the only secretary that had ever been there.

When her chair collapsed two days ago, Dr. Williams had bought a new one. As she sat in the brand-new chair, her attention was focused on the lever at the bottom that adjusted the height. When she pulled it up, it released some mechanism that allowed the chair to slide easily up and down.

Helen was concentrating on adjusting it *just so* because she was convinced that if it was not at the proper height, it would cause her to have bad posture which would lead to back problems in the future. She was intent on taking preemptive measures from the git-go. Her problem at the moment, however, was that she was trying to adjust the chair *while she was sitting in it*, and it kept dropping down to the lowest setting while she tried to balance herself above it, causing her-ta da!-significant pain in her lower back.

As she continued to fight with the chair, now with beads of perspiration popping out uniformly on her forehead, a large man opened the main office door and shuffled toward her. Dr. Williams had specifically forbidden Helen to install any sort of bell or device that would announce the arrival of a patient. He insisted that his office would not be made to resemble a 7-Eleven. This particular edict from Dr. Williams irritated Helen to no end because she was constantly being startled by patients, or the mailman walking quietly to the counter. They would invariably wait until they were in her personal space before announcing their presence with, "Good morning!" at which she would be startled out of her skin.

The man ambling toward her now was very large, although not in very good shape. He shuffled toward Helen-who was still focused on her chair-with practiced short, quiet steps. He was a man who did not like to make a fuss. He noticed that Helen was bent down doing something to her chair and looked very agitated. He thought he heard her mumble something-

sonofabitch!

-under her breath.

The man came to the counter, leaned over it, and said, almost in a whisper, "only name like it in the country."

Helen jumped out of her skin.

"Oh!" she screeched, looking up and placing one hand to her chest, her other hand still manipulating the lever on the chair to adjust its height.

"Oh, Mr. Porter, you startled me!" Helen made no effort to hide her irritation as she straightened up. When she had regained her composure, she addressed him again, this time in her professional voice.

"I'm sorry, what did you say?"

"The name Biloxi," replied Mr. Porter. "There is only one city with that name in the entire U.S. of A, and here we are."

Helen looked at him with a blank stare.

"Well, yes, Mr. Porter, I think that's true. But we're not in Biloxi. We're in Gulfport," she explained, staring him down and waiting for the inevitable look of confusion that always spread across his face when he came in for his weekly appointments.

Helen was not sure of Mr. Porter's particular psychosis, and truth-be-told she really did not give a shit one way or another. She had long ago given up on trying to play doctor to the patients. But there were, of course, the occasional exceptions. Mr. Porter was one such exception. Ever since his appointments with Dr. Williams had begun more than two years ago, he still said and did the oddest things. He was a big man, but not physically imposing, and he could never maintain direct eye contact with anyone for more than a few seconds before looking away.

One of Helen's guilty pleasures in life was to stare down Mr. Porter at least once every time he came in. More than that if she could. This time she did it with glee, directing her frustration with the chair, and of being surprised, toward poor Mr. Porter who just stood there, realizing that he had once again done or said something that was not appropriate.

In Mr. Porter's defense, it was difficult to tell sometimes exactly where Gulfport ended and Biloxi began. They merged along the coast, and if you were not paying attention or had not lived in the area long, you could wander from one to the other without really noticing. But Helen thought it was still odd. Mr. Porter was a grown man. At the very least, he should know where he was. Helen feared that Mr. Porter's condition, whatever they called it, was getting much worse.

Poor man is geographically challenged–

–she thought as she directed Mr. Porter to a chair in the waiting area.

"I'll inform Dr. Williams you are here, Mr. Porter."

Mr. Porter appeared not to notice as he stood there, apparently still deep in thought over his current geographical location.

Helen turned her attention to the front door, toward the direction of the sound of squishy shoes trudging along the smooth floor, announcing another new arrival to the office on this dreary Friday morning. Helen mused that rain was the ideal early warning system. No doorbell needed.

As the main office door closed softly behind him, Dr. Jeff Beauchamp squished his way to the reception area.

"Mornin' Helen," said Jeff, with no umbrella or overcoat, and looking decidedly uncomfortable walking in his wet shoes.

"Well, good morning to you, Dr. Beauchamp!" Helen beamed. At a buxom fifty-three, she was old enough to be his mother.

Jeff smiled and pointed his finger in mock anger. "I told you that you didn't have to call me that. Jeff will do just fine." He looked very young, certainly not old enough to be a psychiatrist, but a psychiatrist he was, and had been for a full six months ever since he was hired by Dr. Williams.

"Well, *Jeff*, you know how old fashioned Dr. Williams is about these things," said Helen.

"Yes, I know. Say, does it always do this? Look nice outside when I'm at home and then rain cats and dogs when I step off my front porch?" Jeff lifted his arms so that his suit coat could drip on the floor as he took it off.

"Yes, that's one of the quaint little things about living here," said Helen, flashing a gaudy smile and positively *flirting* with the young doctor. "In fact, you know that. . ."

Swoooooooooooooooooosssssshhhhhh!!!

Helen was cut off in mid-sentence as her new chair collapsed again into the shortest position, dropping her like a ton of bricks more than two feet straight down, almost sending her sprawling onto the floor. She recovered her balance, giving an icy stare with pursed lips to Mr. Porter as she did so.

Helen was seated behind a low counter, and to Mr. Porter it looked like a hole in the floor had just opened up and swallowed her. One second she was there, the next second she was gone. Helen readjusted the chair and looked around, face flushed, to see if Jeff had seen her fall.

Jeff, who was trying to straighten his tie by looking at his reflection in the polished brass coat rack, appeared not to have noticed. Helen was thankful that no one other than Mr. Porter apparently saw her gaffe. She straightened herself up and then whispered to Jeff, "Dr. Williams said to send you back there as soon as you came in."

"Know what it's about?" Jeff asked.

"Well, I think you're going to be sent on an interesting errand this morning. You'll find out soon enough," Helen said, her composure regained. Jeff detected a note of smugness in her voice that said she knew exactly where he was going and he probably was not going to like it. It was still raining outside and he did not like the thought of going out in it again. But still, it was Friday, wasn't it? How bad could it be?

Jeff exhaled, frowned at Helen, and trudged off toward Dr. Williams's office.

Helen settled into the chair, but slowly and with caution, prepared now for another collapse. She had worked for Dr. Williams for fifteen years. During that time she had interacted with hundreds if not thousands of patients. Most were pleasant and appeared normal; in fact *were* normal and just needed help coping with the pitfalls of life.

A little *psychological tune-up* as Dr. Williams liked to call it.

There were a few oddities, like Mr. Porter, who had serious mental dysfunction, but seemed harmless enough.

But there were also the scary ones.

In all her years working for Dr. Williams, Helen could think of only two patients that she thought of as truly dangerous. That actually *frightened* her. Both were men, but she had actually met only one of them in person.

Those meetings were memorable. One of the things that she recalled very clearly was that, within a few minutes of being in his presence, she felt that something just was not right. She remembered the feeling of the hair on the nape of her neck standing up and tingling. It signaled danger, and it was brought upon by his eyes, which seemed to *bore* into her own. That was the telltale sign with this man. He held a particularly aggressive and personal gaze. It was discomfiting to experience it, and it had put her on edge every time he had looked at her.

She knew that Dr. Williams labeled those patients with ANTISOCIAL PERSONALITY DISORDER or SOCIOPATHIC PERSONALITY who exhibited inadequate conscience development or inadequate impulse control. Dr.

Williams was at liberty to call them whatever he wanted, but to Helen those labels were just so much psycho-babble. She saw them for what they were.

Predators.

Pure and simple.

The one sociopathic patient that she had actually met was charged with a particularly vicious personal assault, although the victim had not died. To Helen's consternation, the defense lawyers that came in to visit with Dr. Williams had the annoying habit of referring to the crime victim as the *complaining witness.*

Helen had always wanted to ask them if, God forbid, their crazy client had seen fit to carve out their eyeballs with a butter knife, would they view themselves as victims or *complaining witnesses*? Thankfully, the number of such cases had been so few and far between that she never really got the chance to launch her smart-alecky question, not to mention that Dr. Williams would definitely consider such cattiness toward the suits to be completely unprofessional.

But in the one case over the years in which a patient with *sociopathic personality disorder* had darkened their doorway, even before Helen had learned the details of his crime she could sense right away when she spoke to him that he was essentially *empty.*

Nothing inside at all.

The patient's name was Karl Keys. Karl was uber-creepy. Helen had confided to Dr. Williams that she was highly uncomfortable being in the office alone with him. So much so that Dr. Williams had to make sure that he or someone else was present when Karl showed up for his appointments. Helen remembered when Karl would arrive at the office. He would always walk in quietly, almost as if he was *trying* to sneak up on her, and then he would just stand there, regarding her for an extended length of time with his flat, soulless eyes.

Every time he came in, his gaze set off warning bells at deep levels of her mind. It was one thing for her to stare down the Mr. Porters of the world, but trying that with dangerous men with antisocial personality, men like Karl Keys for example, was another matter entirely.

The unnerving part was that Karl evoked the image of being a wild animal in a cage.

Only there was no cage.

What Karl had done to that poor girl, the way he had broken into her home and *disfigured* her, was fodder for the local newspaper and television stations. Money and connections could only shield these types of things so far. But Karl was, of course, *presumed innocent* of the charges, no matter what the victim–excuse me, the *complaining witness*–said, and Karl had enough family resources to post a bond prior to trial which allowed him to roam free even though it was clear to nearly everyone that he was a dangerous criminal. In preparation for trial, Karl's lawyer had insisted upon a thorough personality evaluation by Dr. Williams. Since this had to be done in person, Karl had been allowed to walk into the office just like any other patient.

On the first visit, Karl's penetrating stare had quickly cowed Helen into looking at the piles of paper on her desk, among which were his files which outlined his behavioral history and the grisly details of his *alleged* crimes—details that had been tastefully omitted from the newspaper (money and influence had at least been able to accomplish *that* modest favor). The physical presence of Karl in the office had heightened the eerie, almost surreal feeling that Helen had to begin with and made her feel, well…a little bit paranoid to go along with the healthy dose of unease.

As she read through the file, unable to stop even if she wanted to do so, she was sure that he was staring at her. That he somehow knew *what* she was reading, and that he was daring her to do something about it. To *say* something. But as she looked through the file, the only thing she did was become more uneasy.

Almost *frightened* you might say.

As she had continued to leaf through Karl's file, unable to stop despite the weight of his gaze, she had had a moment of clarity. Her mind wrapped around one simple thought: it could have been *me.*

She had internalized the simple fact that Karl Keys (who had in fact not been looking at Helen or paying her any attention whatsoever, but rather lazily contemplating the lobby oil paintings) was a person who *preyed upon other people.* In over fifty years of life, Helen had known that such persons existed, but working for Dr. Williams had brought one into her personal space. It all seemed to boil down to the fact that, in the end, Karl and others like him were just wired that way, and were not particularly picky when it came to selecting complaining witnesses.

Helen recalled shuddering as she read through his file, thinking all the while that the sociopath sitting there in the lobby could have preyed upon her just as easily as anyone else. There were no rules governing such things. The normal codes of social interaction, of empathy, of feeling did not compute in his mind and, when it came down to it, it was just damn creepy having to deal with someone who was not constrained by conscience. They were capable of anything. In their world, all actions were fair game. This made them both frightening and interesting at the same time.

Although Helen had personally met Karl, she had never met the second such patient because of his incarceration. Although this second one was the worst of the lot and came from deep money and influence, he had not even been able to make a bond or see the light of day because what he had done was so heinous. No office visits for him. She had read through the file and had been especially aghast, almost physically nauseous, at the crime scene photographs and had been unable to finish looking at them. Helen was thankful that she had never had the displeasure of actually meeting Walter in person. Walter was a killer, utterly without conscience or remorse. He was by far the most frightening individual that

Helen had ever known about and she was a little apprehensive when Dr. Williams directed her to pull the file this morning before Jeff arrived.

Walter was truly frightening.

And Dr. Williams planned to send Jeff to pay him a visit.

Jeff stood outside the door to one of the corner offices. There was a fancy brass nameplate on the door that announced the office was that of Dr. David Williams, M.D. Jeff rapped lightly on the door and pushed it open. Dr. Williams was standing before a large mirror that hung on his wall–

What does that say about one's psychological state, Doctor? Jeff wondered.

–and appeared to be in the process of choking himself with a tie.

"Helen said you wanted to see me?" Jeff inquired as he walked into the office. Dr. Williams was attempting to tie a four-in-hand knot on a rather expensive looking silk tie, but seemed to have forgotten exactly how it was done. Jeff had not seen Dr. Williams wear a tie since he had started his internship. He was accustomed to seeing Dr. Williams in light, long-sleeved turtleneck sweaters, which was very odd since the gulf coast was extremely hot and humid almost all year round. Dr. Williams kept the offices cool with the air conditioning to keep from having heat stroke while wearing his sweaters.

"Yes, Jeff," said Dr. Williams, finally knotting the tie into a half-assed Windsor. "Have a seat."

Jeff sat down in one of the big, comfortable office chairs. He had acquired the habit of waiting for others to initiate conversation and, without even thinking about it, he waited for Dr. Williams to speak.

Dr. Williams sat down heavily in the chair behind his desk, looking stylish yet decidedly uncomfortable in his suit. Jeff noticed that he at least had the fashion sense to buy a three-button suit coat rather than the traditional two-button variety. Dr. Williams stared at the large file on his otherwise sparsely populated desk. The file appeared to contain a very thick assortment of legal documents.

"Jeff, you're from Florida, right?" Dr. Williams asked.

"Yes, Miami," Jeff replied, wondering where this was going.

"Have you ever heard of the Eisen Company? It's a large trucking firm, but I don't know if they do much business in Florida."

"No, never heard of it."

"Well, it was started by Fritz Eisenbeis, who for some reason shortened the name of his company to just *Eisen*," explained Dr. Williams. "It really is a true American success story. Fritz literally started with one old beat-up diesel truck and turned it into a huge freight hauling company, doing business throughout the southeast."

Dr. Williams then proceeded to tell Jeff the story of Fritz Eisenbeis and the fortune he had amassed in the trucking business. Fritz had married a stunningly beautiful woman named Helen Gardner and they had had two boys, Eli and Mark. Eli took over the business after Fritz retired. Eli bought Mark out, eased him out of the business (by force some say), and Mark moved up north and had nothing to do with the company, or his family in Mississippi.

Eli ran the company from Jackson, married there, and had two children, Walter and Kimberly. Eli's marriage was turbulent and marred by scandal in the Jackson social circles. Eli was eccentric and there were rumors of bizarre behavior at the estate outside Jackson.

Extremely bizarre behavior.

His divorce was particularly nasty and bitter. There were charges of physical and sexual abuse swirling in the courtroom and in the newspapers. His wife, Elaine, left him in Jackson and took the children to live in a large house on the beach in Biloxi.

Dr. Williams took a sip of water and propped his feet up his desk as he continued.

"Elaine began seeing me professionally...let's see...it must have been about twenty years ago," said Dr. Williams, brow furrowed and head tilted up, questioning his own recollection.

"She was quite insane," said Dr. Williams, matter-of-factly, "and it took me only one session with her to wonder about the psychological issues of her two children. You see, it is a peculiar province of the rich to be quite adept and resourceful at masking hereditary insanity. If you're poor, you're crazy; if you're rich, you're eccentric, as the saying goes."

Dr. Williams detailed his involvement with Walter and Kimberly Eisenbeis. Kimberly eventually moved up north and lived with Mark and his family. Walter, the oldest, stayed and lived with his mother, who had grown increasingly reclusive over the years. Dr. Williams had dealt with Walter for over ten years through a series of policemen, lawyers, judges, probation officers and other assorted state and private personnel who had attempted to curb the effects of Walter's increasingly serious mental problems.

Dr. Williams looked at Jeff and asked, "Do you recall the term *Folie `a Deau*?"

Jeff thought for a moment.

"Shared psychotic disorder?" Jeff replied, unsure.

"Precisely," answered Dr. Williams, clearly impressed with his intern's knowledge of the term.

Relieved that he knew what Dr. Williams was talking about, Jeff decided to show off a little. "It's the psychosis that develops in a person who is involved in a close relationship with another, the primary case or inducer, who already has a psychotic disorder with prominent delusions."

"Correct," said Dr. Williams, staring out the window at the rain pouring down on a drab, overcast day.

"Schizophrenia is most prevalent in the primary case and Elaine's was no exception. She was a severe schizophrenic with pronounced dyssocial personality disorder."

Dr. Williams paused, and then said slowly, "*Extremely pronounced.*"

"A sociopath?" asked Jeff.

"Yes, a very frightening sociopath," answered Dr. Williams and, almost as an afterthought, "and she did an excellent job of sharing her insanity with Walter. Kim left in time to avoid irreparable psychological damage, for which I am glad. She was a very gifted student and cellist, but Walter...poor Walter never had a chance."

Dr. Williams told Jeff the story of the end of Elaine and Eli's marriage. From the divorce trial and rumors among the scandalmongers in Jackson, it became evident that there was another woman in the picture. Her name was Phoebe Fontaine. She was a Jackson socialite from a prominent family and also a very attractive woman. Eli became enamored with her and essentially abandoned Elaine and the children to pursue a life with Phoebe.

After the divorce, Elaine moved from Jackson to the coast and began the long process of spiraling down the black hole of substance abuse and psychosis, dragging young Walter with her every step of the way. Toward the end, Elaine became fixated on Phoebe, an obsession that she inculcated quite forcefully upon Walter. It eventually destroyed her.

Jeff listened to the story, fascinated by the details. He had moved to the Mississippi gulf coast from Florida only six months before and had no prior knowledge of the sad tale of the Eisenbeis family. He glanced at the file and noticed for the first time that he had never seen the file in the file room. He was positive because he had looked through them all out of curiosity and to see how a top notch psychiatrist like Dr. Williams keeps files and makes notes during the course of the treatment. He then realized that the Eisenbeis file was kept by Dr. Williams under lock and key in his private files.

"About four years ago," continued Dr. Williams, "Walter murdered his mother at their home just eight miles down the road from here, along Highway 90."

Jeff raised his eyebrows, clearly interested now that the story had progressed from psychosis to a murder case.

"When the police arrived at the house, Walter was in the process of trying to *nail* his mother's corpse to the wooden floor." Dr. Williams discovered that he was secretly enjoying telling this macabre story to his intern.

Jeff whistled. "Holy cow."

"That's right," continued Dr. Williams, "he was using a hammer and the biggest nails he could find." Dr. Williams paused for effect. "But that's not the worst of it."

Dr. Williams leaned forward and took a sip of water from the glass on his desk.

"Walter was not arrested immediately. The only two persons living at the home were Walter and his mother. After

Walter's mania had subsided enough for him to have some perception of what he had done, he fled his house and ended up at one of those home repair superstores on Highway 49 where he was finally apprehended but not before he committed the atrocious murder of..."

At that moment, Helen tapped on the door, peeked in and told Dr. Williams that his wife, Florence, was outside waiting on him.

Dr. Williams stood up, presented himself before the mirror and proceeded to put on his suit coat and straighten his tie.

"Well, the file is right here if you want to look through it. But the long and short of it is that Walter barely escaped a lethal injection because of his mental condition. He is housed at Spring Hill." Dr. Williams collected his umbrella and the top file from the stack of papers on his desk as he headed toward the door. He turned and looked at Jeff.

"There is a section at Spring Hill where they keep the dangerous psychotics. That is where Walter is right now."

Dr. Williams handed the file to Jeff. Jeff took it hesitantly. Dr. Williams was clearly leaving, and Jeff picked up the undeniable signals that whatever shit was rolling downhill was most definitely headed in his direction.

"This is a lab report that came in early this morning," said Dr. Williams, not making eye contact with Jeff, as if something perplexing was happening to his shoelaces and he was required to check it out.

"Walter has been having symptoms for several months. Severe headaches and a few mild seizures. The lab verified a grade IV astrocytoma, GBM."

Dr. Williams let the words hang in the air for a moment.

"Walter is waiting for the results. Normally, with what his trust fund pays us on a yearly basis, I would go there and tell him myself. But my wife's aunt Beatrice passed away and the funeral is this morning and I have a house full of guests from out of town."

Dr. Williams looked anxiously at his watch.

"Just review the report with him and explain the pathology. Tell him that I will be over to see him as soon as I can," said Dr. Williams, making eye contact with Jeff again, "and don't forget to take a photo ID. Helen will fax a letter to Spring Hill and explain to them that *you* are coming, because they are expecting *me*. They will not let you in without a valid photo ID."

Dr. Williams turned toward to the hallway and paused, appearing for a moment to contemplate which was worse, attending aunt Beatrice's funeral or meeting with a criminally insane sociopath for the purpose of informing him that he had an inoperable, malignant brain tumor.

Finally, he turned back to Jeff and patted him on the arm. "Security is pretty tight there, but there's no need to be nervous. Just go report the findings to Walter, answer his questions as best you can, and then tell him I will be over there as soon as I can. It'll be a good experience for you."

And with that, Dr. Williams turned and walked briskly down the hall toward the front door where his wife, who had finally begun honking the horn, waited to whisk him off to attend aunt Bea's last rites.

Jeff stood for a moment in the doorway, holding the file and trying to assess his feelings concerning his newest assignment.

CHAPTER TWO

While Dr. Jeff Beauchamp was trying to figure out the best way to inform his new client that he had an inoperable brain tumor, on the other side of town, Lance Davis stood before his dresser mirror, giving himself the once-over, and making sure his tie was straight. Much like Dr. Williams, he did not particularly like wearing a suit and tie, but there are certain things in life that a man must do. One of them was to dress up in a monkey suit for one's twentieth wedding anniversary.

Twenty years.

Margie was still sitting at her makeup table, applying the finishing touches.

Lance looked closely at his face in the mirror and marveled at the time.

Where did it go?

As he studied his face, he realized that, although he shaved almost every day, he could not remember the last time that he had taken a close look at his own face.

A *really* close look.

Leaning close to the mirror, he tried to recall exactly when he had crossed the line into the land of the middle-aged. Where had twenty gone? Where had *thirty* gone? He could not remember. Looking at his face, he noticed for the first time, at barely forty-two years of age, that he actually *looked* his age. The crows feet at the corners of his eyes, the lines around his mouth that lingered there after he smiled, and the creeping salt-and-pepper around the sides of his head were all exhibits for the prosecution. These were things that accrued slowly, the things that were never apparent until one stopped to notice them. In a mirror, say, as one was getting ready to go out for one's anniversary.

There was the evidence, all right. The imprints of a thousand worries, a thousand joys, a thousand days of wondering what it all means.

Twenty years.

It was a milestone that covered a lot of territory. His thoughts drifted to the highs and lows that had occurred during those years. He reminisced by alternately smiling an exaggerated smile, followed by a frown, and noticing the lines in his face as he did so. Lance realized that the lines would soon become full-fledged *wrinkles*; that at some point he would cross over from the land of the middle-aged into the land of the *old.* Lance continued to make faces to himself in the mirror, watching the lines appear, then slowly disappear after each funny face.

"What are you doing?" Margie asked. She stood in the doorway of the bathroom that connected to their bedroom. She was smiling at him as she watched him make faces at his reflection.

Lance had been in deep contemplation. The sound of her voice startled him. He jumped back from the mirror and turned to look at his wife.

She looked stunning.

"I was just thinking of you, dear," said Lance. This was his standard line in such situations. But this time it happened to be true.

Margie stood there for a moment in the doorway, backlit by the bright bathroom lights. She wore a simple, elegant black sleeveless dress and the necklace he had bought for her so long ago. Lance followed the drop as it plunged down her neckline and fell into the crevice of her breasts. The dress flattered her figure and revealed her bosom, probably more than she had intended.

Lance's eyes were transfixed there.

The Davises had a satisfactory, if sporadic, sex life. But it happened that about every two or three years there was a period of time where Margie was irresistible to him. Lance could not explain why this happened. A hormone shift, maybe. Build-up of stress from work, perhaps. DNA wiring during the springtime? He did not know. But during these periods he walked around with a perpetual hard-on, jumping Margie's bones every time she would allow it. These spells usually lasted for about two weeks until his burst of sexual energy was consumed.

For the most part, Margie enjoyed the attention during these spells, although the constant pawing became a nuisance. She always told Lance teasingly that he was "in heat." Lance had been thinking about Margie all day long and now, looking at her dressed to the nines, she looked positively fetching. He started to stir.

Margie saw the look.

"Don't even think about it," said Margie. She walked past Lance, stopping only long enough to punch him hard in the shoulder with her closed fist.

"Ouch!" Lance screeched in mock pain.

After twenty years she could read his thoughts by the lascivious look on his face. Lance was resigned to the fact that she could shoot him down without him having to actually say anything. That was marital efficiency.

Margie stopped at the vanity, cocked her head to one side and, using both hands, pinned in an earring. She met his gaze using the reflection in the mirror.

"You are going to take me to dinner and a show first, Pepe LePew," Margie said, "and *if* I have a good time, and *if* I get liquored up enough, I *might* think about giving you some action later."

Margie put in the other earring and picked up her purse. Lance smiled.

"How does my tie look, dear?" Lance asked, inspecting himself one more time in the mirror.

"Like shit. But let's go anyway. I don't want to be late."

"Yes, dear."

CHAPTER THREE

Deep inside Spring Hill Sanitarium, tucked away under a wool blanket inside a secure cell, Walter Eisenbeis dreamed. He lay with his eyes half-open, looking up at the ceiling, yet seeing nothing. His clean-shaven head glistened with sweat and his eyes made rapid movements under the thin skin of his eyelids.

In his dream he was a child again.

He was running in a meadow. It was inviting, sunlit and safe. As he walked in his dream, he noticed that it was bordered by a small wood. Yellow and purple flowers sprouted up everywhere. He looked down at a chubby hand (*his hand?*) and saw that it clutched a large wicker basket. He was picking strawberries and putting them in the basket. He saw that the basket was full of big, plump, deep-red berries.

He held up for inspection about every fifth one he picked and then he would eat it, savoring the sweet taste, the squirt of juice in his mouth. The colors were spectacularly vivid.

The sensations he felt were *real*.

He stood still, swallowing the last of a berry before he started to walk again, searching for some more. He looked up and saw that there was a trail that consisted of enormous strawberries. He followed it, picking up the berries and putting them in the basket.

Suddenly, the dream-time in his head changed (how exactly, he was not sure) and he sensed that he was not alone.

As he bent down to pick up another berry, he looked ahead and saw the figure of a woman. She was dressed in a long, flowing, incredibly white dress. She also carried a basket, much bigger than his own. Hers overflowed, and with every step she took toward the woods another strawberry would fall, leaving a trail.

A trail for him.

Mother.

She was laughing, looking back at him, but still walking toward the woods, dropping strawberries every few feet. He smiled at her.

"Take them, Bubby," she said in the dream, and then harder, "take every last drop." His mother had turned around and was walking backward, toward the woods yet still facing him, still smiling at him.

But now something was wrong.

every last drop?

It had grown darker and he had not noticed. The woods, which had looked peaceful and pleasant (*when? just a few seconds ago?*) now looked like a dark place.

A *dangerous* place.

He sensed (in the surreality that one experiences in dreams) that the squirrels and woodchucks had been replaced by unknown and unnamed predators.

If they had ever been there at all.

"Wait!" he tried to say, but nothing came out. He wanted to shout but could not. His heart was beating faster and he seemed incapable of catching his breath. He stood there, frozen and unable to speak. He was so afraid. Mother was walking backward into the woods.

Toward *danger*.

He wanted to warn her, *needed* to warn her but he was now powerless to do anything but stand there quaking with fear. Then, sharp, searing pain on his hand. It was the hand holding the basket.

Aahhhhhhhhhhhhh!

His dream-paralysis gave way and he was finally able to scream. He looked down and saw that the strawberries were *moving*. Somehow they had turned into living things, undulating in his basket. No, not strawberries, not anymore. They had *turned*. He watched through the prism of his childhood mind as the strawberries had somehow turned into black, venomous *scorpions*.

A large one had climbed out of the basket and onto his hand where it had plunged its stinger. The pain was instant and unbearable, but he was unable to release the basket. Frozen in a state of terror, he looked back to his mother, pleading with his eyes.

She was still smiling at him, so close to the wood now. But he saw that her basket, too, was brimming with large, black scorpions. One dropped every few feet, leaving a trail for him to follow.

"Momma!" he tried to say again, but the dream-paralysis was back, and although he could make no sound he *could* feel the poison coursing through his body and multiple, rapid stings on his tiny hand.

He looked at his mother's face again and saw that the largest scorpion had crawled up her arm and had sunk its tail-stinger into her cheek. It stayed there, stinging her again and again, making her face puffy and swollen with poison. She was still smiling at him, but this time he saw that what he had thought all along was a smile was not a smile at all. It was a grimace, the rigor mortis of a walking corpse, animated by nothing more than a dream.

Something caught his eye.

At the place where the meadow gave way to the woods stood another woman. At her feet were wolves, hungry and snarling, nipping at each other, waiting for his mother to finally arrive.

Phoebe

She stretched out her hand and pointed to him.

"Take every last drop, boy," she cooed, "gonna give you *every last drop!*"

Then she laughed, a high shrill screech that melded with the snarls of the wolves.

He knew that it was already too late. He could not drop the basket. He felt the biggest and blackest of the scorpions crawl up the handle of the basket. He could feel their weight as they used the basket handle to crawl up his arm and march toward his shoulders and head. He watched their steady, insect-steps as they mounted his arm but he could not move to shake them off.

He looked at Phoebe. She was laughing at him, taunting him as he felt the sting of one, then another, then another, as they struck him in the temples, over and over.

"Take your medicine, boy," Phoebe said, softly, laughing and pointing at him.

take your medicine, boyyyyyy

Walter awoke.

His heart was pounding and he could not seem to catch his breath. His hands went immediately to his temples. The pain there was black and paralyzing. His right hand was not working for some reason. Walter had a moment of panic when he thought he was having a stroke, but he realized that his hand was numb from having been pinned under his body as he slept. While he rubbed his temple with his left hand, he shook out his right until he could feel the pins and needles sensation.

It took nearly twenty minutes for the pain in his temples to subside to a manageable level. Every muscle in his body had been tensed for who knew how long during his dream, and his shirt, shorts, and bedding were damp with sweat from the effort of fighting through the pain.

Walter swung his legs over the side of the bunk and took the cup of water from the night stand. He sat there contemplating for several minutes. The headaches had grown steadily worse, and this one was the worst yet. Walter had suspected for quite some time that he was sick.

Really sick.

Now, at this moment, sitting on his bunk and deep-breathing through another round of vivid dreams and agonizing pain, Walter realized that he was dying. He could feel something wrong with his head. Something in his brain was killing him.

He knew this because he could no longer climb *the grids*.

Since childhood, Walter had sought solace inside his mind. It had been his refuge since the time he had first learned to walk. Later, as he had acquired knowledge, Walter would spend hours inside his own head, stretching his imagination and climbing the grids. At least, that is what he has always called the lattice-worked pattern he sees when he retreats there.

When Walter was an infant, the grids had been just a flat, checkerboard expanse that had contained his thoughts. He would spend hours affixing ideas or images–or just a simple thought–to the places where the gridlines intersected. They *stuck* there. Connecting to the next intersection was effortless, and in this manner he had learned to read and name objects and shapes. The grids seemed to go on forever, spread out in all directions awaiting activation.

An epiphany occurred when Walter was about four-years-old. That was when he had discovered that the grids went *vertical*. No longer just a flat-lined plane, the grids in his head had somehow developed *depth*. They had become a three-dimensional construct, as wondrous to Walter as the stars in the sky.

He remembered being amazed at how he could swing down and stick things below other things, or connect many things together in a way that would make sense. It had become a rich jungle gym through which Walter was able to solve all the problems in his math book without hardly even thinking about them, or recall the names and events in the plays of Shakespeare which no one else, not even the teacher, could remember without looking them up in the book.

On the heels of his great discovery came another one–virtually no one else could climb their own grids like he could, not even the grown-ups. Mother had told him to not reveal the grids to anyone else.

Take a vacation, Bubby, just take a little vacation to somewhere nice.

That was how she had put it. Take a vacation. This meant that he should miss a question or two, or pretend not to know what the thigh bone was called or the answer to the equation that the teacher had drawn on the board.

But he *had* known.

He had known the answers to all of it; how it all worked, how it was all supposed to work. It was so obvious to him most of the time that his attention wandered to the many things that he had not known. To the things that were more interesting. But in class Walter had not seen the reason to take a vacation when he was the only one who knew the answers.

The thing that had convinced Walter to take a vacation was the day that Frankie LeClerc had cornered him in the boys restroom, flanked by Ronnie Hardwood and Grady Thompson. Walter had just finished washing his hands and had turned around to leave when he walked right into Frankie.

Frankie had shoved Walter in the chest, pushing him back several feet at a time. Each time he shoved, Frankie would mock Walter in a falsetto–

What's the answer to THAT?–

Then he would shove, again and again, punctuating each "that" with a shove that sent Walter backward as the sound of nervous laughter from Grady and Ronnie followed–

Got an answer to THAT, freak?–

Until Walter had been flat against the wall, unable to

back up anymore. Then they were on him. Arms pinned tightly behind his back, they shoved him into the last stall and held his head down in the toilet bowl while Frankie had flushed it.

The question is SWIRLY, freak! What is the answer? Hey, Grady, lookit, the freak ain't got no answer to the SWIRLY question. Ain't so smart now are ya, FREAK?

Frankie had jeered this as Walter looked up at him from the floor, his head a wet mass of fouled hair to go along with the chipped tooth courtesy of the hard porcelain. Frankie had reached down to do something else, but the noise of the door to the restroom swinging open had stopped him. He had simply delivered a vicious kick to Walter's stomach without even looking at the door and then had turned around to walk out. Walter had seen that Ronnie was scared, but Grady had wanted to do some kicking himself. The two of them had just followed Frankie out of the restroom, giggling and punching each other.

Didja see that freak flinch, Frankie? Think he'll figure THAT out? Hahaha

The kick had knocked the breath out of Walter and he had sat on the dirty floor by the commode for a long while before he felt like he could stand. Timmy Parsons had come in, seen what was going on, and quickly left without taking a leak as he had intended. But as Walter had lain there in pain and humiliation, he had whimpered from the kick, but he hadn't cried; nor was he particularly angry.

What he had done was climb the grids.

He had climbed until Mrs. Parsons had heard him whimpering and had come to get him, even though she was a woman and it was the boys restroom.

During the entire time that she had stuck his head under the sink to wash his hair and had walked him down to the principal's office to call his mother, Walter had climbed the grids, fixated on how to solve the problem of this insult. He had settled on a black area of the grids that catered to things that were useful. Things that made him feel good.

Things like *revenge*.

Many things presented themselves for his consideration, some of which would have resulted in serious injury or death to Frankie (and to Grady as well). Walter processed them all, weighing the risks, the likelihood of success, of getting caught, whether it would be worth it to get caught, whether he even cared about getting caught. In the end, as things often did in the grids, the simplest solution presented itself at the top of the intersecting lines.

Walter had waited.

It had seemed like forever, but it was only three weeks. He remembered the layout of the playground, how Frankie and the others congregated in the corner, how an alcove in the walkway between the gymnasium and the main building had given him perfect cover while at the same time providing him perfect line-of-sight. *Defilade* was the word for it.

Walter remembered watching the arc of the flat, sharp rock as it had traveled through the air, the way it had glinted in the sunlight and tumbled almost in slow motion before hitting Frankie in the mouth, shattering his front teeth, splitting his bottom lip, and sending him squealing like a little girl to Mrs. Parsons. Walter had never felt so good in his life, particularly when he had seen the blood dribbling down Frankie's chin. From his hiding spot, Walter had dropped the remaining rocks that he had picked out and honed for the job, and headed down to the library where he was supposed to be. He had smiled as he heard Frankie crying.

At least I didn't cry, Frankie. Need a hankie?

No one had seen who had done it and no one ever got into trouble for it. The bad luck for Frankie was that his two front teeth–his *permanent* teeth–needed to be replaced. Walter had giggled every time Frankie tried to talk in class after the incident while he waited for his set of temporary teeth. Frankie had glared at Walter a few times, but the thing was Frankie was so stupid that he had never suspected Walter as the culprit. Walter had waited only three weeks but apparently this was long enough for Frankie to make no connection between the bathroom incident and a rock smashing into his teeth after being thrown by an unknown person.

Walter had been amazed at this. He had fully expected Frankie to retaliate, and he would have welcomed it. Walter had mapped out a series of escalating assaults in his head. Truth be told he was curious to see if he had correctly anticipated Frankie's response, which Walter had predicted would be another bathroom confrontation.

But no response ever came.

Mrs. Parsons had acted like she felt sorry for Frankie and seemed to shrug off the whole thing as an accident, although she had glanced at Walter whenever she said anything about it, as if to say–

Even Steven now. Everything is all square. No more.

That was the point at which, as far as Walter could tell, everyone stopped talking to him, even his teachers unless they absolutely could not avoid it. In fact, they might have been a little bit *afraid* of him. Walter had spent his remaining time in school climbing the grids with books he got from the library or, later, from the university. By the time he had finished school, Walter had no friends, had never kissed a girl, and had no direction in his life, but the grids had run long and deep.

Walter never shared the grids with anyone after the restroom incident with Frankie, and only showed evidence of them when he needed something or to teach someone a lesson. Like when Tommy had brought out the chessboard–and cheated; or when Dr. Williams insisted that he take tests.

It was better that way.

Walter sat on his bed and rubbed his temples. He tried to climb the grids but kept slipping off into nothingness. Blackness. Things that he should know–that he *knew* he should know–would not come.

They either would not come at all, or came sporadically, as if there were a light switch in his head that turned on the grids, only the switch had a short in it. Sometimes the grids went dark.

For example, Walter knew how to disable the safety features on lots of tools—say, a pneumatic nail gun, for instance. He knew those had to touch something to work, but he also knew how to make it work *without* touching the business end to a surface. He had done it before. But, right now he could not think of how to do it; even though he knew how. It wouldn't come.

It was *frustrating*.

He suspected that Dr. Williams would stop by soon and tell him exactly what the problem was, but it really did not matter. Walter was amazingly in tune with his own body—always had been—and knew that his brain was rotting from the inside out. The texture of his dreams, the pain in his head, and now the loss of the integrity of the grids; all of these things had gotten progressively worse over the last few months. Walter was sure he could not survive it much longer. He was also sure of something else.

He would not allow himself under any circumstances to die inside Spring Hill.

CHAPTER FOUR

It had been several years since the state of Mississippi had decided to allow full scale gambling, and with it came the heavy casino presence along the gulf coast. The casinos, in turn, attracted out-of-state tourists and entertainers. It was not exactly Vegas, but there was usually something interesting going on. Many of the casinos along the coast were small scale versions of their Las Vegas counterparts.

Lance liked to sneak off every now and then and play some blackjack or maybe roll some dice, but he had discovered that the proximity to gambling faded the allure of it. He paid attention to the action nowadays mainly for the entertainment.

The insert in the newspaper featured the goings-on for

the week. It seemed there was always a parade of second- and third-tier acts putting on shows, or performers that had been big in the seventies or even in the sixties would re-surface for the easy shows before the casino crowds. Entertainers like Freddy Fender, Hall & Oats, Blondie, David Alan Coe, the Beach Boys, and Johnny Paycheck always seemed to find their way to the coast.

The only exception occurred at the crown jewel of the coast casinos, the *Beau Rivage*. The *Beau* was comparable to any Vegas Strip casino. The boys in Vegas had sunk over a half *billion* dollars into it and it showed. The place was first class all the way, with large fountains, fancy restaurants and a modern theater.

Margie ogled at the large water fountain in front of the main lobby as she and Lance pulled in behind the line of cars waiting for a valet. The *Beau* was bustling all the time and tonight was no exception. It was close to the Fourth of July holiday, and was in fact officially hurricane season on the coast, but on this day the weather was mild with a light breeze blowing in from the gulf.

Lance killed the engine and they stood by the car as the harried valet made his way to them. Other coast casinos simply gave you a ticket and took your keys. The *Beau* was a little more security conscious and required a name while the valet jotted down the tag number.

Lance and Margie entered the *Beau* through the large revolving door which spun them into the magnificent and enchanting main lobby, complete with foliage and high ceilings. Holding hands, they made their way to the *Coral* restaurant.

Normally, Lance would have chosen to eat at Mary Mahoney's for special occasions. Mahoney's was a coast institution with a colorful history and great food. He had even considered squiring Margie around New Orleans, which was a quick one-hour drive from Gulfport.

But the *Beau* had managed to snag George Carlin for a three-day gig so Lance thought it would be special enough to just do the whole night at the *Beau*. Lance led the way through the throngs of gamblers and vacationers, past the raucous dice tables, the unusually subdued blackjack pit, and the inscrutable pai gow tables. *Coral* was set off in one corner, and when they arrived their table was ready.

The ambience at *Coral* was unique. The four walls of the restaurant were giant aquariums, from wall to wall, floor to ceiling. Exotic and colorful fish swam in a lazy circle everywhere you looked. Lance had never seen anything like it. Margie was impressed.

"You know what Chet said to me the other day?" Lance asked as he perused the menu. Chet was his sixteen-year-old nephew who was learning both to drive and sneer with equal enthusiasm.

"What?" asked Margie, trying to decide on the wine.

"We were driving to Edgewater Mall for haircuts or something, and he cocks his head while he's driving, looks at me and says, 'what's it like being forty?'"

"What did you say?" asked Margie.

"I said it's like being sixteen, only different."

Lance buttered a roll. "Fact is, I really don't know how to explain what it's like being forty."

"What's this all about?" said Margie, putting down the menu to look at Lance. "Is that why you were looking at yourself in the mirror?"

She smiled at him.

"Need some of my wrinkle cream?"

"Very funny."

"You're not forty, dear. You're forty-*two*. *I'm* forty. We're getting old. That's the way things are. Just don't go weird on me."

"Huh?" said Lance, gazing at the fish.

"I said don't go weird on me. Middle-aged breakdown, sports car, teenage girlfriend, all that shit. You start that and I will scratch your eyes out, kill you, and bury you in the backyard."

"Hey, a little G&R." Lance perked up. That was one of his favorite songs to play for Margie when he was in a foul mood.

"See, you're not that old."

"Yeah, but *Guns n' Roses* faded away in the eighties, didn't they?"

"I don't know, Lance. The point is that we have it good. Quit being so mopey. It's a great night, this meal is going to be excellent, and I am going to order a bottle of wine for both of us. Well, mainly for me."

"Okay. You're right." Lance did not seem convinced.

But she *was* right. He had been spending a lot of time with Chet lately. No particular reason, really. He just liked the kid. Lance saw himself in Chet in many–and sometimes unexpected–ways. One of the consequences of spending so much time around Chet had been a surprising and powerful bout of nostalgia.

Lance's own high school years were both turbulent and glorious. His experiences during those times were much more powerful than college, and later his work. Spending time with Chet brought it all back, and with it came the realization that he could not, as the old song went, go back again. Those years, those feelings were lost forever. They existed only in his memories now, and sometimes in the increasingly rare conversations he had with long-time friends about the old days. It was depressing.

"Besides," said Margie, taking a sip of wine and snapping Lance out of his thoughts, "everyone will be over in a few days for the Fourth."

Lance groaned. He had forgotten about that. They had volunteered to host the festivities this year.

"Shit, is there no way to get out of it?" Lance whined, knowing full well there was in fact no way to get out of it.

"There is *not*. Besides, you complain about it every year but always end up having a good time. Don't you want to see David and Kim?"

Lance just grunted, signaling his defeat. Margie was right (again). It always seemed like a huge pain in the ass to get everything ready, but he usually did end up having a good time and, when it was over, he was thankful for having so many people who cared about him. He was lucky and grudgingly had to acknowledge it. But it was so damned much work.

"Frank wants to go out and do something before the weekend." This was more of a question than a statement. Lance looked at Margie, waiting for some signal concerning the likelihood of approval.

She frowned.

"Not this weekend. Lance, you are going to help me get ready. If you have to do it, go out on Thursday. But Friday morning I am getting your ass up to help me. Understand?"

Yes!

Lance tried to look defeated while smiling inwardly.

"Okay, okay, I'll help you on Friday."

It was shaping up to be a good week.

The meal was delicious. Lance had a steak and Margie had some sort of seafood sampler platter loaded down with a little smidgen of everything. As they cleaned off the last of the food from their plates, Lance noticed that the wine bottle was just about empty. That was also a good sign. Margie was bound to be in a very good mood. A very *pliable* mood, one might hope.

Lance paid the bill and they walked out into the endless bustle of the main casino floor of the *Beau*.

"I'm going to step into the ladies room," said Margie, giving Lance a quick peck on the cheek.

"Okay, we have about twenty minutes. I'm going to order a drink and wait right here."

The bar was situated in front of the entrance to *Coral*. Lance ordered a Maker's Mark and Coke with a long pour thank-you-very-much. He took a sip and shivered. *Damn.* That was a good, strong drink. No skimping at the *Beau*.

As he stood there sipping his drink, he looked out onto the casino floor. Closest to him were a row of blackjack tables flanked by endless rows of slots. Further down was the craps pit and even more slots. One of the blackjack tables closest to him was empty, manned by a lonely dealer standing behind the table outlay and looking bored behind a pile of six decks of cards arranged with a flourish on the table.

Lance had an impulse.

He checked to make sure Margie was still in the ladies room. No sign of her.

He walked over to the empty table.

"Good evening, sir," said the dealer, who had seen Lance walking over and had already started shuffling the decks and placing them in the shoe.

"Good evening to you," replied Lance, reaching into his pocket and peeling off three bills from his wad which was bound by a collage of multi-colored rubber bands. He placed the bills on the table inside one of the wager squares.

"Play it," he said, singing a little jingle in his head.

Dinner and a show was going to be on the Beau.

"Playing three hundred," said the dealer loudly to the roving floor man who glanced at the money and then at Lance.

"Do you have a player's card, sir?" asked the floor man.

"No," replied Lance.

"Do you want one?"

"Not right now."

The floor man nodded at Lance and then to the dealer.

The dealer held the huge stack of cards in his hands and offered Lance a bright yellow plastic card with which to cut them. Lance took the card and placed it near the top. The dealer finished the cut where Lance indicated and then placed the cards in the shoe. With practiced efficiency, the dealer dealt the cards, one up and one down for the house and both of Lance's cards face up.

Lance's first card was the jack of diamonds and second was the beautiful ace of spades.

Blackjack!

The dealer's up card was an eight. He flipped up his down card, revealing a ten. Eighteen. Not good enough. The dealer then counted out four black chips and two green chips from the center racks–four hundred and fifty dollars–and placed them on top of Lance's three bills.

Lance picked them up, tossed a greenie to the dealer, and walked back to the bar just in time to catch sight of Margie emerging from the ladies room. It was five minutes to showtime and the restrooms were getting full.

"Let's go have some fun," he said, draining his drink. Between the wine at dinner and the drink he downed while playing the hand of blackjack, Lance was getting a little bit tipsy. Plus, the extra cash in his pocket put a spring in his step.

"What's gotten into you?" asked Margie, looking especially radiant.

"Just having a great time with my lovely wife," replied Lance as they walked toward the show room where Carlin awaited.

Carlin was a riot. Lance had seen him a few times on television, but in person he was much better. He came out for an encore and brought down the house with a bit about how he would balance the federal budget. *Carlin-style.*

As they filed out, Lance could not recall having a more perfect evening. The whole day had been fabulous and it was not even over yet. Although he did not know it, it would be a very long time before he would feel that good again.

Because, in only two more days, he was going to meet Walter Eisenbeis.

CHAPTER FIVE

Jeff drove north along Highway 49, toward Spring Hill Sanitarium, glancing every few minutes at the passenger seat where he had placed Walter's file and, on top of that, the lab report. It was not good. Walter had a brain tumor and it was one of the worst. A Grade IV GBM Astrocytoma was malignant and aggressive; a very nasty tumor. Jeff had time to conduct some quick-and-dirty research before the visit and he pondered the best way to tell the bad news to Walter.

Probably better to just be blunt.

The mammalian brain is highly specialized. Each part of it makes a unique contribution to the whole, even on a cellular level. Although the human brain remains largely a mystery to medical science, there have been great strides made in mapping it. Certain areas of the brain are understood to a significant degree. In Walter's case the tumor was attacking the frontal lobes. Jeff noted with concern that damage to some sections of the frontal lobes could result in profound changes in behavior, including emotional affectations, impulsiveness, distractibility and, in Walter's case, a pronounced reduction in ethical restraint. Jeff recognized that this was academic-speak for saying that Walter, already a dangerous sociopath, was about to become even more so.

Jeff pulled into the main entrance at Spring Hill which opened up into a large parking lot. He surveyed the area and saw that the parking lot was separate from the facility. He was going to have to walk to an electronically controlled gate for admittance. Wicked looking coils of concertina wire snaked along the fence line in both directions. More disconcerting was the fact that he could not see a single person inside the perimeter, nor could he hear anyone.

Technically, Spring Hill was not a prison; rather, it was a mental health facility. Jeff wondered about that. He sensed very little treatment was going on here.

He collected his materials, stuffed them into his briefcase and then navigated thirty yards up the sidewalk to the gate. An intercom was mounted to the right and he pressed the button.

"Help you?" The voice was female, and irritated.

Jeff leaned into the box.

"Jeff Beauchamp to see Walter Eisenbeis."

"Appointment?"

"Yes."

Jeff stood there for what seemed like a very long time. From his vantage point he could see the main administration building through the fence. It was another thirty yards straight ahead. He was about to push the intercom button again when he was distracted by a loud popping sound coming from the administration building. It was the sound of heavy metal being released by some powerful mechanism.

The formidable front door of the building had opened and a uniformed security officer was walking toward him. A woman. Jeff looked beyond her and could see the heavy glass surrounding what had to be the main control room. Inside he thought he saw another female form.

The irritated one no doubt.

His escort was dressed like a soldier in combat fatigues, but armed like a police officer: clipped at various places along her black utility belt were a semi-automatic Glock 9mm handgun in a holster, heavy steel handcuffs, extra magazines for the Glock, what appeared to be a mace canister, and on her left was an elongated riot baton swinging to and fro on her hip with each step.

She stopped when she reached the inside gate. There was an electronic buzzing sound as the heavy gate in front of Jeff slid on its tracks to his left. When there was enough space for him to squeeze through he took a step inside the holding area and waited for the gate to slide back into place. When it did, the inside gate was electronically opened and the escort turned around and started walking back to the building, motioning for Jeff to follow.

He did so with the noise of the closing gate following him up the sidewalk.

Inside the administration building, the white walls glowed in harsh light. The escort directed Jeff to the main control window which acted as the reception area for official (non-family) visitors.

A steel-barred man-trap was set in the wall across from the front door.

"All yours," said his escort to a figure inside the glass-encased control room. She walked out the front door, leaving Jeff standing there and without ever having said a word to him.

From inside the control room, another officer appeared. She grabbed a microphone, pressed a button and spoke into it.

"Beauchamp?"

"Yes." Jeff was beginning to feel very small.

"Any weapons or other contraband?"

"No, ma'am."

"Sign-in and waiver," she said, pointing to a clipboard on the counter. Jeff looked at the forms. The top one was a simple sign-in sheet. He grabbed the ancient ballpoint pen affixed to the clipboard and printed his name, the patient's name, the reason for visit, the date, and the time.

The form underneath was titled "Waiver of Liability." It was a solid block of cramped legalese in small print with a signature line and place for the date underneath. Jeff considered not signing it, but knew that if he didn't sign, he would not be allowed to see Walter.

A thick metal drawer opened with a loud clang beneath the window, making Jeff jump. This place seemed to be designed specifically to create random loud noises. Jeff wondered if anyone could ever get used to it.

"Empty your pockets and put the contents in the tray. Everything goes in the tray. Driver's license and keys on top."

Jeff felt like he was being manhandled, but he complied and put all his possessions in the tray, including his briefcase which barely fit. As he placed his driver's license and car keys on top of the briefcase, he had just enough time to pull his fingers back when it slammed closed again.

The woman inside rummaged through the case, removing paperclips from his painstakingly organized file.

"Hey, don't lose those papers!" Jeff cried.

If she heard him she did not show it. When she had removed all the clips from the case and completed her inspection, she closed it and placed it back in the tray.

"Here you are, Mr. Beauchamp," she said, returning the now-scrambled folder inside the case. Jeff saw that she had placed a clip-on visitor's badge on top of his case. The badge had a number on it, but no name.

"Put that on and keep it on at all times. Do *not* lose it. Take off your shoes and have a seat over there. Someone will be with you in a moment." She paid no attention to Jeff's irritated stare as she turned around and tended to something else.

He took the badge, clipped it onto his lapel and removed his shoes. He marveled at the gruff manner in which they treated him. He was a medical doctor, here on official business.

Wonder how they treat the patients.

Jeff re-ordered the papers in his folder as he waited. He did not wear a watch and there were no clocks in the room. After an undetermined but very long time, he heard a loud buzzing sound from the man-trap.

Upon closer inspection, Jeff saw that the man-trap actually resembled a tiny jail cell with four walls of horizontally spaced steel bars, except that two of the sides were electronically controlled, steel-barred sliding doors which blocked access to a long hallway where the inmates (*patients*) were housed. Anyone going back that way had to wait for the door to slide open, step into the cage, and then wait for the door on the opposite side to slide open before they could leave.

As Jeff looked at it and how it operated, a large athletic-looking male guard emerged from it. He had come from the side that housed the patients. As he ignored Jeff and walked to the control room, Jeff noticed that his name tag said JONES.

To Jones, the officer in the cage said, "He's here to see Eisenbeis. Shake him down and then take him back."

Officer Jones nodded, already checking to see if Jeff had taken off his shoes and directing Jeff to stand up and spread out his arms for a patdown. Jeff did so without protest and was patted down just like he saw on television when someone was being arrested. Officer Jones did this in a purely perfunctory, professional manner, but Jeff found it insulting nonetheless.

When it was finished, he put his shoes back on, gathered his case, and followed Officer Jones, who had started walking back toward the man-trap without saying a word. The two of them waited for it to open and then walked through, with Officer Jones in the lead.

Jeff was not normally claustrophobic, but the ordeal of going through all the security measures had him feeling a little bit closed in. The inside of the man-trap was small to begin with, but being inside it with a larger man made Jeff uneasy.

It seemed like it took forever for the man-trap doors to cycle before they could emerge on the other side of the hallway. Jeff was glad to get out of the cage and walk again. He followed Officer Jones. When they had walked about twenty feet, Officer Jones slowed down to look at Jeff. He had figured Jeff for a first-timer at the institution and waited for the look-back as soon as the door slammed shut.

It happened every time.

Jeff was no exception. When he was waiting in the lobby, Jeff had not really paid attention to the loud closing noise made by the electronic door as it slid in place. Then, of course, he was free to walk out the door if he wanted. But as he walked twenty feet down the corridor, the door slammed very loudly behind him and he stopped to turn around and look at it. Now, it blocked his way *out*.

Jeff realized that he was now trapped *inside*. It caused him a moment of hesitation, and to look back to the door. He contemplated it briefly and then turned around again to follow Officer Jones, who turned with him and led the way.

They walked down another hundred feet to an unmarked door which Officer Jones opened with a key from his belt. The room was bare, containing only a table–which had deep gouges in it from some long ago, unknown display of aggression–and two chairs.

"Do you have your visitor's badge?" Officer Jones asked.

"Yes," responded Jeff as he tried to settle in one of the chairs, "but what happens if I lose it?"

"*Don't* lose it."

Officer Jones turned to go retrieve Walter, then closed and locked the door, leaving Jeff inside to sit and wait.

About ten minutes later, Jeff heard the keys rattle outside. The door opened, and Officer Jones escorted Walter into the room. Jeff had seated himself against the far wall so he could face the door as it opened. Walter's frame was huge as he shuffled into the room and sat down in the opposite chair. He was dressed in blue-jeans and a tight-fitting, white t-shirt, as well as leg irons and a belly chain which curtailed his range of motion. Officer Jones waited for a second to take direction from Jeff as to whether he should remove the shackles. Typically, a professional visitor would ask for that, but Officer Jones could see that Jeff was not going to be in charge of this meeting.

Officer Jones nodded toward Walter but looked at Jeff, "We'll leave those on for now." He pointed toward a speaker on the wall that had a metal button under it. "Push that when you're through." He then walked out of the room, locking the door behind him.

When they were alone, there was an awkward (for Jeff at least) silence before Jeff stood and offered his hand to Walter, stretching it out over the table.

"Hello, Walter. I'm Dr. Jeff Beauchamp."

The gesture was appreciated. It had been a long time since someone had extended to Walter the courtesy of a simple handshake. He stretched out his hand as far as the belly-chain would allow and shook Jeff's hand, applying a great deal of pressure to the squeeze. Jeff appeared not to notice and sat back down, going immediately to his case to pull out the paperwork.

"Where is...uh..." Walter stated, frowning as he struggled to recall the name.

"Dr. Williams?" Jeff inquired.

"Yes, *Williams*. Where is he?" Walter had no actual interest in the whereabouts of Dr. Williams. The fact that he had sent this kid over instead of coming himself was a sure sign that whatever news was going to be given would be very bad news indeed. Walter had always regarded Dr. Williams as a chickenshit, and this just confirmed it.

The troubling part was that Walter had forgotten his name. It was something that he should have been able to remember.

Jeff removed some papers from a file and placed them neatly on the table. He looked up at Walter.

"Dr. Williams actually had to attend a funeral today. He said that he would be over to see you as soon as he could."

Walter did not reply to this.

Jeff moved on. "The reason he sent me here is that we received the lab results. I suspect that you are accustomed to frankness so I will just tell you straight away. Walter, you have a very aggressive, and inoperable, malignant brain tumor."

He awaited a response from Walter, but got no visible reaction.

"It's called a Glioblastoma Multiforme, Grade IV, which means that it grows very fast and is very aggressive. These infiltrate the brain very quickly. The symptoms that you have already reported should probably have progressed further, and other symptoms will develop as the tumor grows. You should be experiencing such things as bad headaches, possibly seizures, memory loss and behavioral changes."

Jeff was uncertain whether he should continue, but Walter nodded in silent assent.

"As the tumor progresses, so will the intracranial pressure. This may lead to clouding of consciousness, disorientation, carelessness in personal habits, irritability and sometimes sensorimotor loss."

Jeff stopped at this point.

He considered telling Walter that the tumor would also likely have a *pronounced reduction in ethical restraint*, but considered that for a man who had murdered his own mother and who had *nailed* a woman to death in a hardware store, it was a little bit redundant.

"Are there any treatments?" Walter asked. It came out more as an inquiry of whether there was any hope at all.

Jeff frowned, dreading the conversation. The information in the file had steeled him to despise Walter. Jeff had in fact thought of it as hardening his heart against Walter almost in a biblical way.

Yet, in the confines of the tiny room, when he was actually face-to-face with the man, Jeff found that it was very difficult to muster righteous indignation, or to take any pleasure in telling this man the bad news. Walter's flat affect was evident, but there was no outright menace in him at the moment. Jeff's mind wandered momentarily, and he thought that his lack of hate somehow reflected more on his own character than Walter's. He absentmindedly went through a quick thought process on the implications of this before noticing that Walter was waiting for a response.

"Treatments?" Walter said steadily.

"The way the tumor is situated in your brain, surgery is just simply impossible. The only viable treatments are radiotherapy and some form of chemotherapy. In fact, we would want to start those as soon as possible."

Walter's eyes grew wide at this and, for a split-second, Jeff saw abject fear in them before Walter quickly brought both hands to his face, rubbing his eyes and temples. Walter rubbed fiercely for about a minute before looking–almost peeking at Jeff–as a child would after having been frightened.

Walter was also breathing heavily. As Jeff was talking, Walter had seen a large black scorpion tail uncurl from behind Jeff, then raise up in the tiny room, a droplet of venom hanging precipitously from the monstrous stinger at the end. It was coiled to strike when Walter frantically brought up his hands to rub his eyes and temples. Up until this time, he had felt coherent, and the headaches had tapered off. Now, they were starting up again in earnest, just behind his right eye.

The sight of the stinger had sparked the fight or flight reflex in Walter before he realized that it was not real.

Could not be real.

Walter regained his composure.

"How long do I have?"

"It was caught early, but to be honest with you, Walter,

you will be lucky to make it two years. Most do not make it that long, although there have been rare cases of patients surviving these types of tumors for three years. Our best guess is less than two years."

Jeff considered and then added, "I'm sorry."

Walter did not reply to this. He had heard enough. Heard what he *needed* to know, at least. Walter rose from the chair, turned around, pushed the call button below the speaker, and stood there waiting. He regarded Jeff.

"Thanks for coming."

"Do you want to see the report?"

"No," replied Walter, "I think I know the situation now."

Jeff did not believe that he did. Jeff stood up, afraid that Officer Jones would come back and escort Walter out before he was able to finish his last bit of business.

"The medical transfer is already in the works. Dr. Williams submitted the paperwork last week to the lawyer–I'm sorry I forgot her name–and I believe that she indicated that you would be transferred very soon to a minimum security facility as a result of your...terminal condition."

Walter considered this, amazed that the parasitic Dr. Williams had actually come through with something helpful. He was not surprised that his lawyer, Pamela Chain, had been able to accomplish the transfer. Walter had liked her from the beginning.

She was almost like him.

"What does that mean, exactly?"

Jeff looked at the file. "According to this letter from the lawyer," Jeff glanced at the letter, "Ms. Chain...since you are here under court order, your incarceration falls under the rules of the Department of Corrections. They have a set of rules governing placement of terminally ill inmates. Technically speaking, Walter, you are eligible to be sent home. Ms. Chain did not think that was possible given your...*situation*, but she can make sure that you get moved to a private facility with much less security and no perimeter. It requires the approval of the Chief Medical Officer here, but Ms. Chain believes that is doable."

Walter smiled.

He had paid both Dr. Williams and Pamela Chain's law firm a fortune over the years (or, to be more precise, the administrator of his financial affairs had paid them). He had no doubt that Dr. Williams's report was tight and professional, and that Chain would have no problem convincing that hack Dr. Sibley to go along.

Chief Medical Officer, my ass.

Dr. Sibley had more problems than most of his patients here. Walter doubted it took much pressure from Chain to get that little task accomplished.

For the first time in a very long time, Walter relaxed a little bit.

Things were looking up.

Officer Jones arrived, gave a perfunctory knock on the door, unlocked it, and led Walter out without any more conversation.

Walter did not look back or say goodbye.

Alone now, Jeff gathered up his file, mentally trying to assess how he felt about this meeting. He unconsciously shook his right hand out in front of him. It was the one Walter had shaken when they had met. One thing was for sure. Walter was *strong*. He had just about crushed Jeff's hand, but at that point Jeff realized that it was just Walter establishing control of the meeting from the outset. Jeff resolved to not play that game or to give in to it. Still, the strength was impressive. Jeff pondered a while longer, almost convincing himself that Walter was *not* playing games with the handshake.

Then he smiled.

Not going to get inside my head, my friend. Not today.

In the end, he discovered that he was happy to see Walter leave, and even happier to be escorted out of that horrible place.

CHAPTER SIX

Lance awoke feeling absolutely shitty.

The night before, he had gone out with Frank Henderson and Carl Sanders (under the unspoken protestations of Margie). The night had started off on the wrong foot when they had decided to eat at a new mom-and-pop seafood place along the coast called *The Sea Urchin*. Good seafood was really good, but bad seafood was really, really bad. By the time they had settled up, the fish had not settled well with Lance-or with Frank-but Carl had proclaimed his meal to be one of the best that he had ever eaten.

Since Carl was feeling fine, actually *more* than fine, by the time they had left, he directed them to what he had called a "gentlemen's club" (a titty bar, as Chet would say) where Lance ended up drinking much more than he should have.

The titty bar was named *Cat Calls*, and it was what substituted for class on the coast. A twenty-spot for a cover charge kept out most of the riff-raff and, as always, the girls followed the money and the men followed the girls. The place was not that large, but it did not need to be. Three small stages were dispersed throughout a sea of comfortable chairs. The place was packed. Cigars were apparently the order of the day. The smoke was thick once they arrived, but Lance noticed that the ventilation system seemed to work adequately once they had been there a while.

Just as Lance was getting his second lap dance from a beautiful dancer named Stormy, he realized that the fish he had eaten earlier in the evening at *The Sea Urchin* was bad. It hung in his stomach like a radioactive lead ball, as if it was sitting there contemplating just how bad it wanted to fuck him up.

Of course, he came to this realization only after he had drank way too many Maker's Marks, way too fast. As Stormy gyrated slowly in his lap, Lance was dimly aware that he was poisoned by both food *and* booze. This made him laugh.

What a *riot*!

It was all good. At *Cat Calls*, the lap dances were a bill each, and you did not even venture onto pervert row without having at least fivers to dole out to the dancers. No singletons in this place. The dynamic made everyone happy. The money attracted the best girls and the girls in turn attracted the men with the money.

Stormy and her friends were quite enough to direct Lance's attention away from his stomach and his impending hangover.

Cat Calls was, if nothing else, a huge vacuum cleaner which sucked up money faster than it could be taken from thick wallets and greasy hands. Frank ran low first and Lance and Carl followed quickly thereafter. By then it was nearly closing time at two in the morning.

Lance was at a table talking to Stormy and another dancer named Passion. Passion had a tattoo on her left breast and Lance was trying to make out what it was, but could not focus on it in the dimly lit room.

Passion popped the breast out of the nightie she was wearing and pushed Lance's head close to it.

"It's two unicorns fucking," she said matter-of-factly.

Lance stared at it from about six inches away. Slowly, the image appeared in his head, like a Rorschach test image that clicks in place after contemplating the ink stains. Lance roared with laughter.

"Hey, Frank, come check this shit out!" Lance yelled.

Frank ambled over with Carl in tow. Each sat down heavily in the two remaining chairs. Frank took a huge chug of his *Coors* regular (he refused to drink light beer, proclaiming that such swill was for pussies), and squinted his eyes in order to get a good look at the tat.

Passion held still for inspection, although she appeared bored already. Stormy put a dainty hand to her mouth, stifling a yawn. It was closing time and the money to *be* made had already *been* made.

"You see it?" Lance asked, not wanting to give away the secret.

A smile spread on Frank's face. "Hey! Hey! That's two horses fuckin'!"

"Not two *horses*," said Lance, "two *unicorns*."

Lance and Frank guffawed in tandem, while Carl just looked at the girls and smiled. They were obviously ready to go. Carl looked around as the lights came on. It appeared that the bouncers were coming around to kick everyone out. Carl thought of the old bar saying.

It's closing time, you don't have to go home, but you can't stay here.

Carl had been nursing ice water for the last hour in contemplation of having to be the driver on the way home. He was on probation at home also, and did not want to rock the boat by coming home shitfaced or, even worse, getting arrested for a DUI and *then* calling home from the county jail shitfaced.

"Looks like we gotta go, boys," said Carl.

As if in agreement, and with the final word, Passion covered her titty tat with her nightie as she and Stormy got up and walked away, blowing kisses to Lance and Frank. The other patrons were making for the exits and the dancers were making for the back. It was indeed closing time.

Carl guided Lance and Frank outside and to the car. As they fumbled along, Carl thought that Frank was in blue-ball heaven, but Lance did not look so good. Probably just overdid it a little bit in there. Well, he'd sleep it off soon enough.

They piled into Carl's Buick and headed down the road. Carl dropped Lance off first.

"See ya at work tomorrow...I mean this morning!" Frank yelled as they drove away.

As Frank's laughter drifted away into the balmy coast evening, Lance made his way to his front door, fumbled around with the key and, as he opened the door and stepped inside, his head started swimming with alcohol spins accompanied by an ominous trembling in his bowels.

He made it into his bedroom, took off most of his clothes, and plopped down hard into bed next to Margie who seemed oblivious that he had finally made it home. He passed out.

After a fitful four hours, Lance awoke at six-thirty with a head-splitting hangover, a slight fever, and a very bad case of diarrhea. He detected the aroma of freshly brewed coffee, signaling that Margie was awake. He stumbled into the bathroom where he spent a good twenty minutes ejecting liquified shit from his outraged middle-aged digestive system. He sat on the throne, sweating and with his left arm clutching his stomach which was cramping now.

Jesus, how did I end up like this?

When the cramp-wave passed, he sat for a while longer just in case there was a surprise. There was not. He cleaned himself up and then stood and looked at his face in the mirror.

He looked terrible.

This is what haggard looks like.

Margie came in the bedroom as he was getting dressed, a hot cup of coffee in her hand which she set down with a glance of mild reproach. It smelled really good, but he did not think it would be wise to drink it in his current condition. He reconsidered and then drank it anyway.

"Thanks."

"Don't think just because you're draggin' ass that you can get out of helping me this afternoon," said Margie as she walked out of the room.

Lance made no reply. He managed to dress himself and make it to the kitchen. In the fridge he found some Pepto and drank about a quarter of the bottle. He then walked down the hallway to the bathroom where he looked around in the medicine cabinet and found some Tylenol. He took two, washing them down with coffee, then decided to take a third for good measure. Lance grabbed his keys and headed to the door.

"I'm leaving, be back early this afternoon," Lance yelled to Margie. No reply. No kiss goodbye this morning, either. She was in a mood.

Lance thought about how he was going to make it up to her, but the first order of business was to make it to the office. He opened the front door and walked out to his car, energized by the promise that, because tomorrow was Independence Day, there was only a half day of work scheduled. Even in the shape he was in, he felt like he could manage it.

Out of there by noon, baby, with a full weekend of recovery ahead!

That was the plan.

CHAPTER SEVEN

At Spring Hill Sanitarium, around the time that Lance Davis was splashing his toilet bowl, Officer Tommy Jones was getting more than a little nervous. He glanced around again at the empty bed on "D" wing with mounting unease. Walter was not in his room. He was not *anywhere*. This was not good.

More than that, it was downright frightening.

Tommy grabbed his radio and keyed the send button. "Harvey, any sign of him?"

Harvey's voice came back on Tommy's unit. "Negative. He ain't here, man. Walter has flown the coop." Tommy clipped his radio handset back to his uniform.

Shit.

Harmon, his supervisor, was not going to be happy about this. Not at all.

If only it was anyone but Walter–

Tommy thought. Anyone but him.

The thing was, it just did not make any sense. Walter was going to be transported from Spring Hill to a private nursing facility in Jackson. For all practical purposes, this was *freedom.* This was also the reason why Tommy had let his guard down a little bit. Nothing bad. Just a little bit of extra freedom for Walter since he was going to be transferred this morning, a transfer by the way that Officer Tommy Jones thought was *nuts.*

Walter Eisenbeis had been a "patient" at Spring Hill for four years. Four long years since Walter had been declared criminally insane by the court and committed to the care of the State. Walter was technically still going to face trial if he was ever deemed sane, but that looked like something that was not going to happen now. Tommy could have told the judge that it was apt to be a long wait. The main reason being that, in Tommy's estimation, Walter was an incurable homicidal maniac. Tommy was no doctor, but he knew *crazy* when he saw it.

And he knew *dangerous* crazy when he saw *that.*

Walter was dangerous crazy. Tommy had been a guard at Spring Hill for a long time, and had interacted with hundreds, maybe thousands, of criminally disturbed minds.

But Walter…*did things.*

Things that just were not normal, especially during the last few months. Walter could sometimes make the hair stand up on the back of Tommy's considerably large neck just by looking at him. He was sure that the young doctor had sensed it, too. Walter had flat eyes. Most of the time, there was no remorse in those eyes. Tommy was quite sure that if Walter were to, say, cut out your heart and feed it to you one piece at a time, he would exhibit the same facial expressions and pulse rate as if he were discussing the weather or doing a particularly easy crossword puzzle.

Walter was committed at Spring Hill for two murders, but Tommy suspected there were others for which Walter was simply never caught. But the two were bad enough, especially the one at the store. That poor woman. As Tommy stood in Walter's room, trying to figure the current situation out, he recalled the details. He remembered vividly when it happened because his uncle George had been a police officer at the time and saw firsthand the result of Walter's handiwork.

As Tommy recalled, she was just minding her own business, shopping at some big store, the *Builder's Emporium* maybe, when ol' Walter well…just went nuts, right there in the middle of the store. Somehow he had armed himself with a pneumatic nail gun and was just standing in one of the aisles when Amy Holmes came walking toward him, looking for the lumber department. There was a large stack of plywood right behind Amy as she had walked by Walter, not paying any attention to him.

Walter had pushed her hard up against the wall of plywood and began to busily *nail* her to it.

Several brave employees had actually tried to help Amy, but were met with zipping nails, *big ones*, and two had to receive medical attention for their wounds. By the time the police arrived, exceptionally fast in this case, Walter had nevertheless managed to drive over *three hundred and thirty* large nails into Amy's screaming, writhing body.

The first officer on the scene approached Walter with gun in hand and saw him pulling the trigger of the then empty nail gun as he aimed it at a scarecrow leaning against a stack of plywood. As the officer approached, he gasped as he realized that the scarecrow *attached* to the wood was a woman.

Walter was screaming, "NOW, PHOEBE, *NOW* YOU FINALLY HAVE TO TAKE *YOUR* MEDICINE!" Over and over he called Amy Holmes "Phoebe" and exhorted her to take her medicine. Other officers arrived shortly thereafter and subdued Walter with unexpected ease. The only reason they did not kill him then was because he had run out of nails and had no other weapon.

They dragged Walter through the *Builder's Emporium* while he screamed non-stop about Phoebe and the fact that she needed to take the rest of her medicine. No one at that time knew who "Phoebe" was or why Walter thought that she needed to take her medicine.

Tommy really didn't give a shit, either. He had more immediate concerns. Walter was not only crazy *dangerous*.

He was crazy *smart*.

Just after Walter had arrived at Spring Hill, Tommy had rummaged around the recreation room one day and found an old chess set. It was a cheap one with light plastic pieces and a black-and-red checkered board.

Tommy had been studying the game with his nephew and considered himself a *playa*. He had looked for a chess set because the patients had been getting restless and bored. An activity was needed. Tommy had the idea of organizing a chess tournament. Competition always made things interesting, even in the nuthouse. He had been astonished to learn that most of the patients seemed to know how to play, and some were pretty damn good. The tournaments were held after lunch in the recreation room, and at first they were a hit.

But, after the first week, interest faded because of Walter. No one could beat him. Not a single time. Most everyone stopped playing after a couple of weeks because it was pointless whenever Walter played. Even Walter got bored with it because no one could give him a game.

But the thing that had spooked Tommy was the way Walter had played. Although Walter sat down at the chess board when the tournament started, by the middle-game Walter didn't even look at the board. He read magazines or newspapers while someone called out the move using the standard chess move conventions. Without looking at the board or seeming to stop reading, Walter would simply call out his move.

And he never lost a game playing this way.

After observing this, Tommy had set up the board at his station where Walter could not see it at all. Tommy had shouted out the moves to Walter and Walter responded with a move of his own, playing blind the entire game and keeping track of the moves in his head. Tommy never won a game playing that way.

Undeterred, Tommy had brought a handheld computer chess game to work one day. He had gotten it from his nephew who used it for practice. Tommy was not proud of cheating with the computer, but even on the highest setting not even the computer could checkmate Walter. Most of the games against the computer ended in a draw; and Walter was playing them blind while doing something else.

The one time that Tommy thought he was going to be a winner against Walter was a game in which Walter seemed to play giveaway with his pieces. Tommy had felt a pang of guilty triumph as Walter's pieces dwindled down to a bare king, which Walter walked into a corner of the board behind some of Tommy's pawns. Tommy still had a rook and two bishops and was–with the help of the computer–about to deliver checkmate on the next move.

But the next move was Walter's. Tommy had seen that Walter was not in check, but that he had no legal move to make since any move would put him *in* check.

Stalemate

Which in chess is considered a draw. Walter had

laughed at Tommy in a way that Tommy did not like. "Better get a stronger engine, Officer Jones," he had said. The computer game had gone back to the nephew and that was the last of the chess games.

But Walter's intellect was not just devoted to chess. His perception was keen in other areas. For example, he could tell when someone needed a little financial assistance from time to time. In fact, Tommy himself often needed such assistance.

It had started out with little things.

One day Walter had a craving for a Snickers. He had not had one in years and could not obtain one at the commissary at the Hill. Walter casually mentioned to Tommy that he would pay twenty dollars just to taste a Snickers. Maybe even thirty or forty. Tommy got the message and did the math. Buying candy bars for a dollar and selling them for forty was a pretty good deal.

From then on, Walter always came to Tommy when he wanted a little favor here and there. Snickers bars had been the bait. When Tommy had taken it, Walter had revealed the real prizes: books. Walter needed books.

The Hill had no formal library. The only reading material consisted of periodicals and books that had been donated. For some reason, the donors were overwhelmingly old ladies, which meant that the reading selection at the Hill consisted of *Reader's Digest*, books on gardening, and pulp romance fiction.

Walter was being stifled.

Tommy had ended up providing all sorts of books to Walter over the years, some of which he had to special order. Walter liked textbooks on all subjects, but particularly in the fields of medicine and psychiatry. Tommy suspected that he was self-diagnosing. During the last year or so, Walter's interests had shifted to pure mathematics.

After the chess debacle, and during a period when Walter was deep into a book on cosmology, Tommy had taken a peek at Walter's file. Strictly speaking, Tommy was not supposed to have access to it, but professional courtesy existed at the Hill.

Most of the reports in Walter's file were difficult to understand, and a lot of the documents were legal. But Tommy never forgot the page that described Walter's IQ test. It was a computer generated form that listed the actual score–which did not mean anything to Tommy–but to the side was the result expressed in terms of percentile of test-takers:

> 99.999 (SD:16)

Walter's score was better than nearly everyone who had taken the test. Tommy had also noticed handwritten comments by this last part. Someone had written "ACCURATE?" in block letters, and then below that was a reply in different script: VERIFIED by DLW.

For the most part, Walter had just wanted books. When he had asked for other favors, Tommy had been willing to go only so far. He would not do anything to get anyone hurt, and certainly would never grant any favors that might allow Walter to escape–not that Tommy cared what Walter would do if he escaped, but if it happened then there would no more favors. That would be bad for business.

Tommy liked Walter right where he was.

Not that it mattered. Tommy always figured that in the larger scheme of things, Walter's incarceration was not his call to make. If the doctors and the lawyers wanted to let Walter do his stint at some cozy hospital in Jackson rather than at the Hill, then it was on them if (*when*) Walter wigged out.

But while Walter was still a resident at the Hill, it was Tommy's problem. He went back over it in his head, trying to come up with a rational scenario.

He still could not understand it. Early this morning, Tommy and Walter had been loading up the transport van to go to Jackson. Walter had wanted a little bit of air before leaving on the trip. "Free air" as he had called it. That's it. Tommy had not thought that the request was unreasonable.

Walter had not breathed "free" air in over four years. What could be the harm? Especially when Walter was basically home free anyway. It never occurred to Tommy that he would try to escape *now*, when he was, for all intents and purposes, just a few hours from that goal. It made no sense in Tommy's mind.

You askin' about what makes sense to crazy *people?*

"Yeah," Tommy said to himself.

"Harvey?" Tommy spoke into his radio handset.

"Copy," Harvey replied.

"Call Harmon. *Right now.*"

CHAPTER EIGHT

Half the battle for Lance was getting to the office on time. The other half was trying to hide his hangover and then trying not to shit his pants while he was there.

For Lance, work took place on the fourth floor of the Kennedy Building where the administrative offices of Petra Energy were located. It was a small cap company, but had thirty-two full-time employees, headed by Mr. Armand Petravich who was in Europe for the holiday. The office staff consisted mainly of geologists and accounting folk. Lance had been there long enough that he actually did a little bit of both. On this fine morning, however, he was in no mood to do either.

He was met at the door by Bruce Rigsby. Bruce had a passing resemblance to the comedic actor Rob Schneider, which was enough for Frank to christen him Deuce Bigelow, which in turn was later shortened to just plain Bruce the Deuce (although usually Frank changed it again to Bruce the Douche). Bruce the Douche was the kind of guy who actually volunteered, *fucking volunteered*, to work during the holiday weekend. There was no effective response to such brown-nosing tactics. No one else volunteered, but it made everyone else a little bit uncomfortable because no one knew exactly how old man Petravich viewed such things. Lance and the others just held their collective breaths, hoping that the old man was old *school* and recognized a greasy suck up when he saw one.

Bruce began Lance's day by proceeding to break his balls about some spreadsheets from four years ago that Bruce had asked Lance to find last week. Lance had been unable to find them, and did not have them this morning. Bruce quickly sized up Lance's condition and frowned.

"I can't do much this weekend without those, Lance," said Bruce.

He let the statement hang in the air for a moment before shaking his head sadly and explaining that he might have to ask the office manager, Steve Jarrett, to find them. Of course, Frank had christened Steve Jarrett with the moniker Jarret the Ferret, although that was not really fair to Steve. He was not a bad guy and was a pretty good boss overall. Bruce was prattling on about how he was *quite confident* that Lance would be able to find what the company needed by the weekend, and that if he could not then Mr. Jarrett would have to find them himself.

Lance despised the way that Bruce casually made such a threat, as much for the way it impugned Steve Jarrett as an office hack (which he was not) as for the way it was an attempt to squeeze Lance. Still, it was a little bit weird that the data could not be found.

Judas priest, didn't they keep that shit in accounting?

It was, after all, four-year-old data, but it was not in the place where Lance could have sworn he put it, and it was not in any of the files on any of the computers or the server.

"Chill out, Bruce. I will find it. I have already spoken to Steve about it and he said that it can wait until Monday." Lance smiled inwardly at the hesitation on Bruce's face at this last bit. It had clearly never occurred to Bruce that Lance would go to Steve *first* about the matter. Lance had executed a little preemptive strike and it had had the desired effect. Bruce sauntered off without another word and Lance was delighted to see him go.

Lance hightailed it to his own modest office and plopped down heavily in his chair behind his desk. He resolved to actually deal with this problem on Monday. But for now, Lance considered himself a clock-watcher and it was time to get some more Tylenol and start watching the clock. Old man Petravich had ordered the office closed at noon and it could not get here soon enough. Lance tidied up his desk and thought about how to survive until noon. Perhaps a raid on the break room would be necessary. There was usually some Pepto in the fridge (at the very least some chewable tablets in one of the drawers), and always some Tylenol or aspirin somewhere in the cabinets.

Not to mention some water. He was dehydrated and had cotton mouth.

As the day slogged on, Lance was concerned that he might not make it. His head was fine thanks to the copious amounts of Tylenol that he found in the break room (it helped with the fever, too), but his stomach was messed up and neither the Mylanta nor the Pepto seemed to be working. He had had several bouts of severe stomach cramps all morning and it did not seem to be getting better. However, the clock-watching was going swimmingly and Lance cheered as it inched closer to noon.

His office door opened and Carl popped his head into the room without knocking.

"Hey, peckerhead, you look like shit," Carl said cheerfully.

"Yeah, I *feel* like shit, too. Say, didn't that fish make you sick? How can I feel this bad and you not?" Lance asked.

"Because I didn't have the fish. Don't you remember?" Carl replied.

Crap. I guess I don't remember.

Lance did not have the energy to argue with Carl. Come to think of it, Lance had never seen Carl take a sick day in almost three years. Carl was apparently impervious to sickness, and evidently could handle his liquor as well. In fact, he looked quite chipper. Lance had an idea. Perhaps he could bluff Carl into using some of his boundless energy to find the lost data.

"Hey Carl, Bruce wants the spreadsheets from four years ago. You know, the ones we talked about and I..." Lance was cut off immediately as Carl shook his head.

"Ohhh, no, no, no, my friend. You are *not* going to lasso me into *that* shit. It is thirty minutes until four days of drunken debauchery and I could give a *shit.*" Carl was animated.

Lance was quiet and decided to just sit there and rub his temples. He was not going to get anywhere with this today.

Carl waved it off and continued, "Hey, I came here to tell you a funny as shit joke I heard last night."

"Frank told it to me last night at *Cat Calls* and I nearly fuckin' died laughin'." Carl was grinning and gesticulating with his hands. Must be a good one.

Lance leaned back in his chair, brought up his hand to his forehead and, with his thumb and forefinger, began to massage his temples. "Okay, what is it?"

"This is great! Okay, listen, there was these two teenagers. They came home late from a date to the girl's house. Check it. Her parents are home, but they sneak into her bedroom. They're about to get it on when the guy says, damn, I have to go to the bathroom. He starts to walk out the bedroom door when the girl says, Wait! The bathroom is right by my parents' room, you can't go in there or they will hear you! She is panicked. Can you go in the kitchen sink? The guy thinks for a minute and says fine. Okay, says the girl, you go and I will keep watch. They sneak quietly into the kitchen, which is dark, and the guy does his business while the girl keeps watch. Are you done? she says. Almost, says the guy. *Could you hand me some toilet paper?*"

Carl cackled with glee and clapped his hands. "Get it? He was actually taking a *shit* in the..." Carl was one of those people who felt compelled to explain a joke to everyone fifty times to make sure that they got it.

"Yes, I fucking *get it,*" said Lance, still rubbing his temples. Although the more he thought about it the funnier it became, and he soon found himself laughing along with Carl.

"That was pretty good," Lance said absently as he stared at his watch.

"I thought so, too."

"When did he tell you that? I don't remember it."

"I think you were too busy getting serviced by Passion."

Lance tried to remember.

Carl ignored him. "Okay, I got one more then I'm Audi."

Lance twirled his hand in the air. *Get on with it.*

"Okay, a guy goes in to see the doctor and the doctor says, sorry but I have *bad* news for you and *worse* news. The guy is distraught, but says okay let's hear the bad news. The doctor says, the bad news is you have cancer. Oh shit! Says the guy. What is the worse news? The doctor says, the worse news is you have Alzheimer's. The guy wipes his forehead and says, whew! At least I don't have cancer!"

Carl went off again, fingers splayed out in front of him, "See? He forgot about the cancer because he has the Alzheimer's!" Lance could not help laughing, mainly at Carl.

Carl turned toward the door, "Hey, I'm outta here. If you want to do something this weekend, give me a call. Later." And with that, Carl was gone. As Lance watched Carl leave, he wondered where Frank could be. Lance had not seen Frank all morning.

Lance managed to get out of the office by noon without incident. On the way home, he stopped at a quick shop, bought some Imodium A-D because the Pepto just was not cutting the mustard, and then he headed home to complete the one chore that Margie had assigned to him, which was to mow the yard before all the relatives came over to tear up their house.

CHAPTER NINE

The Builder's Emporium sat off highway 49 in a huge lot next to *Pepe's Pizza*. The *Emporium* was one of those modern monstrosities of corporate America which operated on the principle of offering *everything* for sale under one roof. If a man wanted to build say, a modern three story house, he technically would be able to find all the materials necessary to do so inside the *Emporium*. It had all the materials and tools needed to build...well, damn near anything you wanted to build.

Lance Davis had been there many times, although he was not there at the moment. He thought of the *Emporium* as the home builder's answer to a *Wal-Mart Supercenter*. Lance had wandered around a cavernous *Supercenter* one time and recalled thinking that, if he were somehow locked inside of it for five years, he would be able to survive just fine. It contained plenty to eat, television, music, reading material, games and puzzles, tools, clothes, bedding, even jewelry. It seemed to Lance that nowadays modern life boiled down basically to building a house using materials from the *Emporium*, and then filling it up with stuff from the *Supercenter*.

On this morning, at about the time that Lance was driving home from work, Heidi Beckman, one of the teenaged checkout girls at *The Builder's Emporium*, at first could not believe what she had just heard over the radio. She took a step closer to the cheap radio that she had on all the time at her checkout station (much to the chagrin of one Martin Mathers, the store manager) and turned it up. The radio announcer repeated the story.

The voice announced, "Again, this just in, it appears that Walter Eisenbeis, the notorious Nail Gun Killer, has escaped from Spring Hill Sanitarium where he has been held for the last four years. Officials say that they do not know at this time how he escaped, but that he should be considered armed and extremely dangerous. Eisenbeis was convicted of the gruesome murder of a local woman with a nail gun at *The Builder's Emporium* four years ago. Anyone with information concerning his whereabouts is advised to immediately contact the Harrison County Sheriff's Office. In other news..."

Heidi turned it down again.

Damn, that is spooky.

"Hey, Angie, did you hear that?" Heidi asked.

Angie Choate, manning checkout register number five next to Heidi, turned around and said, "Hear what?"

Heidi glanced around the almost deserted store. Upon seeing no one around, she said in a loud whisper, "That guy that killed that woman *in this store* is loose!"

"Loose?"

"Yeah, he *escaped* from the nuthouse this morning! I just heard it on the radio! Holy *shit!*"

"Cheryl, come here!" They both said this almost simultaneously, beckoning the only other cashier on duty, Cheryl Rainbolt, to come over and be informed of this juicy bit of news.

All employees knew about the Amy Holmes murder. The first thing a new employee was shown was the very spot where Walter had nailed Holmes to the load of plywood. It was a rite of initiation of sorts. Heidi, Angie and Cheryl all knew exactly where it had happened over on aisle Nine.

It had been creepy ol' Purvis Cooper (or "Purvis the Perv" as they liked to call him behind his back), the Lumber Department foreman, who had shown each one of them where it had happened when they had started working at the *Emporium*. Purvis had solemnly walked them to aisle Nine and pointed out a dark spot on the floor. He told them that it was a bloodstain of the Holmes girl that the police could not remove. None of them believed it (well, *mostly* did not believe it) of course, but still, it *did* kind of look like it might be blood. But the cops had labs and stuff to clean all that stuff up nowadays, right?

Escaped lunatic or not, it was getting real close to closing time, right before a holiday (a four-day weekend holiday no less), and all three girls were more than eager to get the heck out of Dodge. They were all still in a group talking about Walter's escape when Randy Philpot came up from the back of the store and said, "Hey, let's get those registers ready to close and police your stations."

Police your stations?

All the girls thought that was the most dweebish phrase they had ever heard. Randy was the Assistant Manager at the *Emporium* and that was his pet phrase. When he wanted one of them to pick up trash, sweep, or tidy up the checkout area, that is what he would always say.

Police your stations, ladies.

On this day, however, instead of policing their stations, the three girls simply looked at Randy, trying to gauge whether he had heard the news about Walter. From his good mood, they judged correctly that he had not. They all figured that if anyone would have a reaction to the news, it would be Randy.

When the murder of Amy Holmes happened, *Emporium* upper management in New York referred to it as a "very unfortunate incident, not associated with *The Builder's Emporium* or any of its fine products." But Randy, for one, associated the incident with his employment in a powerful way. In fact, Assistant Manager Randy Philpot had been at work on the very day of the murder.

On the day it had happened, Randy had been driving a forklift on the other side of the store at the same time that Walter had gone nuts. Randy had not been able to hear much over the noise of his lift, and in fact had gone way in the back of the store during the whole thing. He had emerged only when the police were carting Walter off, who at that time was screaming incoherently as he was led away. Randy had given a report to the police about what he had done during the incident, but that was all.

No one knew that on that day Randy was able to get a good long gander at the Holmes woman before her body was taken down from the plywood stack and removed by the medical examiner's office. In the confusion surrounding the capture of Walter, there had been basically no one tending to the deceased. Randy, in fact, had come upon it by pure accident as he had been walking down the aisle from the back of the store, curious (but cautious) about the loud screaming.

At first he had thought that the store was being robbed, or that maybe they had caught a particularly obstreperous shoplifter (which happened more than most folks might think). As Randy had walked toward the murder scene, Casey McKee, another lift operator, had come up to him and told Randy excitedly that the cops "got the guy" and that everything was under control.

But as Randy had walked down aisle Nine toward the front of the store he had come across Amy Holmes still nailed to the plywood stack.

Everything definitely was not under control, thank you very much.

Randy's pace had slowed from a brisk walk down to a slow walk, down to slow motion steps, to finally complete stillness as he had stood by himself looking at the senseless horror that had just occurred. Amy had looked like she had been almost...*crucified.* Her arms had been pinned by huge nails at nearly ninety degree angles on either side of her body. He had noticed sporadic nails along her legs which had pinned her denim jeans taut against the plywood backdrop and had held her body in place.

But the worst part of the scene was her head.

Walter had aimed the nail gun and shot her face until it became almost unrecognizable. It had looked like a mass of nails that had been driven into a pack of sirloin steaks and then covered with tufts of long blond hair. Had she made gurgling sounds or had he imagined that part?

Randy had stood there, stunned, for what seemed like a very long time, but in reality was only about ten seconds. His mind had perceived the body as a large doll rather than a human. He had stood there looking at it, actually trying to rationalize the horror in a way that his mind would accept, until a police officer had approached and made him clear the area. The officer had explained to Randy that the area was a crime scene and that only law enforcement personnel could remain there.

Randy had never really come to grips with what he had seen that day. He could not afford to quit his job–in fact he loved his job–but working in the same place where such a horrifying event occurred had proven to be difficult for him. New York, God bless'em, had offered to pay for professional counseling for employees who thought that they needed it. Randy was the only one who took advantage of the offer because he *did* need it. He was, in fact, over four years later, still working through some *issues*.

The cashier cadre, although aware that Randy was sensitive about the Holmes murder, did not truly appreciate the depth of feeling that the event had had on the man; but they sensed that upon hearing the news he would have some sort of a reaction. This was why, as the glorious four-day holiday weekend approached, his gaggle of cashiers was staring at him silently as if his fly were open.

"See something green, girls?" Randy asked, starting to feel a little uneasy about the way they were looking at him.

"Huh?...Uh, no, Mr. Philpot," said Heidi, unsure of what the hell he meant by seeing something green (*what does that mean, anyway?*) and uncomfortable about telling him the news. "We just heard on the radio that the crazy guy who killed that lady here escaped this morning."

"*What*!?" Randy cried, eyes wide with surprise and visibly shaken.

"Yeah. They said he escaped and is dangerous and they haven't found him yet," said Heidi.

"Isn't that *freaky*?" Angie interjected. "I mean, what if he *comes back here*?"

Angie emitted a tension-filled laugh at this last part.

Randy tried to absorb this bit of nasty news. Although a cold spike of fear ran through him, he kicked his brain into manager mode and proceeded to think about what they had just told him.

Looking at Angie now, Randy said, "Did the radio *say* that he was coming here, Angie? I can't imagine that we would not be notified by the police if that were the case."

Angie replied, "Well, no, but it's still freaky." And then in a voice pleading a little bit more than she had intended, "I'm ready to go, Mr. Philpot."

Randy considered this for a moment, then raised his head, firmly in command, "Now girls, come on. There's no reason to believe that that nut is going to come here. That happened a long time ago. But it is getting close to quitting time, so police up your areas and let's get ready to go."

That is exactly what they did.

Randy walked away quickly, going back to his cubbyhole office in the back of the store to get his paperwork in pristine order *toot sweet* because, no matter what he told the girls, he most definitely wanted to get out of there as soon as possible. There was, of course, no reason to believe that–

what was his name? Eisenberg? Eisenstat?

–the guy would come to the store. But still, Angie was right. It was downright *freaky* just the same. Randy looked around on his way to the back of the store. There seemed to be only two customers in the place and, in his personal opinion, the sooner they vacated the premises the better.

He was ready to close shop.

CHAPTER TEN

Mowing the yard.

Lance hated it on a good day, much less on a day when he was reeling from multiple poisonings. But it was, of course, the one thing that Margie wanted done. His promise to *actually do it* had smoothed the way for the night out with Frank and Carl. Begging off for medical reasons related to said night was out of the question. His only option was to limp through it in the hopes that when he finished he could then collapse in his bed for a long, shitless sleep.

The riding mower usually made it a good deal easier, but not on this day. The noise would be the worst, but he would get through it. No weed-eating. Just mow the grass.

That was the plan, and it was doable.

When he had arrived home from the office, he had quickly changed into some shorts and a t-shirt and then went out back to the storage shed.

Damn, it was hot.

He checked the oil and gas levels on the big Sears Craftsman riding lawnmower, sweat already beading on his brow and falling from his nose as he checked the fluids. Plenty of both. Lance wheeled it out, climbed aboard and, like the ignominious captain of the Exxon *Valdez*, headed for disaster.

He actually completed the front yard without incident, other than the noise making his head pound like a piece of iron being beaten against an anvil. He drove around to the backyard without stopping, and actually made several swathes around before the Craftsman made a low, belching sound and the grass stopped coming out of the side chute.

He had run over something.

Shit on a fucking stick.

This could not be happening. Lance had been deep in thought, trying to think of where he could have stored the missing data at work, when he felt the mower shudder and come to an abrupt halt, giving him a mini-whiplash.

He looked down with dread at the blade casing and saw that he had run over the water hose. The hose still connected tightly to the spigot by the house, but it was pulled taut between the spigot and the Craftsman, the last ten feet or so wound up tightly in the blades of the mower.

Should have never gotten out of bed this morning

Lance thought as he assessed the predicament in which he now found himself. He was almost finished with the yard. That was the pisser. Just a few more swipes and then blessed sleep.

How the fuck did I not see it?

He resolved to simply untangle the hose from the mower blades, finish up, and then crash. His stomach was starting to rumble and cramp again. That was the plan until Margie came around the corner of the house and saw what had happened. Lance became aware of her presence and looked up. He did not like her look.

"What?" Lance asked plaintively.

"Well, I was just coming back here to get the water hose, *dear*," Margie said with a slight smile developing from her full lips.

"Well, I..." Lance began, but just petered out as he watched Margie place both hands on her hips, unintentionally displaying her cleavage beneath her thin work shirt.

"You, *what*?" Margie asked, needling him more for going out to the titty bar rather than for running over the hose. Margie knew that he felt ill and thought it was, well...*just*. He should receive his proper punishment for staying out all night looking at other women.

"Lance, you know we have the whole family coming over here tomorrow and I need that hose to finish washing the cars, watering the flowers and trees, and washing off the driveway." Margie was actually beginning to feel a little sorry for the poor sumbitch.

"Besides, we need that hose and another one also to mark the boundaries for the volleyball game."

Shit. He had forgotten about that.

"Don't we have more hoses in the shed?" Lance asked, trying to maintain a semblance of hope.

Margie informed him that, no, they did not have any more hoses in the shed; they'd lost them all in the move and had not bought any more, *except* for the one that she'd bought that he'd just destroyed with the lawnmower and, further, that he had better get his hungover-ass up to *The Builder's Emporium* before it closed and buy *two* long water hoses so they could have a proper afternoon of family fun on the Fourth of Fucking July.

Lance could say nothing. Margie stood there, hands on hips, challenging him to lodge a complaint.

After twenty years, Lance could sense when there was no use in putting up a fight, and at this point there was no defense. He accepted his defeat. Margie was a good woman. By and large she let him have his fun without too much of a brow-beating. She had, in fact, God bless her, let him off the hook easy today with the sole responsibility of mowing the yard (not even weed-eating, just mowing the grass for Christ's sake) and he had fucked up even that simple chore.

There was no defense.

He felt her eyes scolding him about how maybe he should spend more time at home eating dinner with his wife instead of with those two degenerates at work, and maybe pay more attention to his wife's tits than those on the floozies down at *Cat Calls*, and maybe if he did those things then horrible things like waking up with a hangover and diarrhea–and possibly running over garden hoses–would not happen to him.

Lance could not argue with *the look*.

He got down off the mower and walked toward the garage to drive to *The Builder's Emporium* for more garden hoses.

"I'll be back after a while, Margie. I think I may stop by the office to check on something on my way back," said Lance, thinking that maybe he might know where those data sheets were after all.

Hell, he might even stop by and one-up Bruce the Deuce.

Margie, a look of triumph in her eyes, simply said, "Don't be too late, *some* of us have work to do."

Yes, dear.

CHAPTER ELEVEN

Lance drove about three blocks before he realized that the air conditioning in his car had given out.

It was kind of funny because Lance cranked that mother on *full tilt* with the windows all the way up. There he was, in his car in the middle of one of the hottest summer afternoons with the windows rolled up and the fan, on high, blowing the hottest air in the world directly on him. With a whimper, he rolled down all four windows using the electric buttons on his driver side console.

Good God!

His sweat from mowing the yard had returned and was already beaded up on his brow, ready to drop. His pits were sweltering under his shirt. For an awful moment Lance was afraid he was going to simply overheat and faint. He had come close to doing it years before and the feeling was the same.

But now, driving along with all the windows rolled down, the breeze actually felt good, even though the air was still incredibly hot.

Fuck, it's like a little vent straight from Hell.

Then he realized that he had rolled down the windows but had failed to turn off the fan which steadily blew the hottest air in the world directly into his face. Lance quickly snapped the fan control knob to the OFF position and wondered absently how all of the freon had gone out of his A/C.

It was at about this time that Lance approached the turn-in lane to *The Builder's Emporium.* He pulled in and began to search for a parking spot. The problem was not cars; the lot was essentially barren of cars. But for some reason most of the parking lot had been roped off for some sort of repair. A re-painting of the parking lanes from the looks of it. Lance was forced to park an eternity away from the front door, almost by *Pepe's Pizza.*

Lance parked the car and killed the engine. With a severe headache from the heat and his hangover, a case of rumbling intestines, trepidation about the lost data sheets, and a feeling of dread over the impending invasion of his home by his relatives, Lance Davis walked to the front doors of *The Building Emporium* marked ENTER, not knowing that his day was about to get a whole lot worse.

CHAPTER TWELVE

As Assistant Manager Randy Philpot walked back to his office to prepare a hasty departure from the premises, Lance Davis stepped through the sliding glass doors of *The Builder's Emporium* and into the merciful coolness of the cavernous building. The air inside felt refreshing against his face after his hellish ride, which was followed by a furnace blast of heat from the black asphalt when he exited his car in the parking lot next to *Pepe's Pizza*.

He may survive this day after all.

Randy did not notice Lance's arrival. The three remaining checkout girls also did not notice Lance because they were huddled around the radio at Heidi's station, trying to gather some more intelligence on the escaped Nail Gun Killer. When Randy had walked away, Heidi had turned up the volume so they all could hear it.

Once inside, Lance made a beeline to the Gardening department. He walked straight up aisle Three, took a left, and spied the vast supply of garden hoses, displayed like benign green snakes that had curled up to sleep.

Christ, how many different types of garden hoses did they make?

Lance marveled as he stood there assessing exactly what kinds of hoses he needed. He did not recall hearing Margie say that she needed a specific color or length, but now it appeared that he was going to have to make a decision and he certainly did not want to fuck this up too. That would be disastrous. At the moment, Margie was still in relatively good spirits. She had had a little fun breaking his balls before he left but hey, he fully deserved it and he knew it. No cryin' by Mr. Lance Davis.

But *shit*, who knew that a man could have so many choices in garden hoses?

Fortunately, Lance had a good recollection of the one he had run over with the Craftsman and he located that model on the shelf. He was actually reaching for it when there was a rumble in his stomach, coming in great waves, followed by severe cramping in his lower belly. His balls tightened and tried to crawl to sanctuary up into his abdomen.

Lance knew that he had to make it to the head, and fast.

He wheeled around, garden hoses banished from his thoughts, and spied the universal sign for men's and women's bathrooms straight ahead.

Thank God.

He finally caught a break. He hunched over, cradling his lower stomach with his right hand, and short-stepped awkwardly toward the facilities. His conditioned worsened after a few steps and his balls actually began to *ache*. Lance was in a precarious state of flux, and had to walk cautiously toward his destination, one careful step at a time.

"Comin' through, comin' through, *it's touchin' cotton here*! Comin' through!" Lance mumbled under his breath as he finally grabbed the door handle and entered the men's room.

By the time he reached the silent sanctuary of the last stall–the big one at the end that was reserved for the handicappers–the situation was red alert critical. Lance closed and locked the door, turned around and, after one horrifying moment when he thought that the zipper of his shorts had gotten stuck, assumed the position.

CHAPTER THIRTEEN

In addition to Lance, who was securely tucked away in the men's room, there were still two stray customers inside *The Builder's Emporium*. Both ambled up at the same time to the cash register manned by Heidi. She had been trying to look busy so they would not come to her station. She wanted to listen to the radio for another update on the status of Monsieur Eisenbeis. However, when it became apparent that they were carting their crap to her station, she turned down the radio and readied the magic wand that scanned the UPC codes on all the items in the store.

Heidi assessed the situation.

The first customer in line was an old man who had a

single item–a pair of gloves. Behind him was a middle-aged woman with a cart containing miscellaneous items, including a large barbecue grill. Heidi looked down at Angie and Cheryl, who were standing in front of their stations silently laughing.

Angie's station was clearly marked the EXPRESS CHECKOUT station, for fuck sake. Why, Heidi wondered, would these dumb animals wander over to her station? *Both* of them no less, when there were two other stations open, and one of them was clearly marked EXPRESS CHECKOUT. Heidi wondered if the old bastard would be smart enough to figure out how to put the gloves on his hands.

"Good afternoon, sir. Did you find everything okay?" Heidi asked in her best perky checkout girl voice.

As Heidi scanned the gloves, Randy walked up, looking antsy. "Anyone else in the store, Heidi?"

Heidi glanced up at him, feeling the old man staring at her perky teenaged tits as she did so, and said, "No, this is it."

She was irritated. She was the only one in the store actually *working* and naturally Randy the dweeb had to ask *her* about other customers in the store. What had she done to deserve this? Angie and Cheryl laughed out loud this time, unable to contain themselves as they looked at the frustration mounting on Heidi's face.

Randy said, "Okay, make the announcement and let's get out of here."

He carried a large stack of documents over to the SPECIAL SERVICES station and began to shut it down. After the middle-aged woman finally carted her stuff out of the main doors and into the parking lot, Heidi grabbed the microphone, gave Angie and Cheryl a snotty look, and then made the announcement.

"Attention customers. The Builder's Emporium is now closed. Please make your selections and proceed to the check out counter."

Heidi thought that the announcement was idiotic when there was no one else in the store, but Randy insisted on it as "store policy."

She was *so* ready to get the hell out of Dodge.

CHAPTER FOURTEEN

Lance had been sitting on the industrial strength commode for aeons. Just when he thought that he had finished, there would be another rumble from his bowels and tightness in his balls. At last, it seemed that the Imodium A-D was kicking in. He sensed a truce developing between his last meal and his digestive tract. A loud chirping sound snapped him out of a rather pleasant daydream. The sound seemed to come from a ten pound cricket and echoed loudly off the walls of the men's room.

Lance looked to where the sound was coming from and reached down to pick up his cell phone. He had forgotten he had the damn thing clipped to his jeans. He glanced at the caller ID and saw with alarm that it was the number to the office. He considered not answering it.

It was probably just Bruce calling to break his balls about the data sheets. But, then again, maybe it was Steve Jarrett. Lance weighed his options. Bruce the Douche could brown nose and *talk* about breaking his balls. But Steve Jarrett, well...he had the authority to engage in some *actual* heavy duty ball breaking. Lance thought that he had made a pretty good preemptive move, but maybe something had gone haywire with it. Reluctantly, he answered it on the fifth ring right before it went to voicemail.

"Hello?" Lance spoke out loud. There was no microphone that he could see on the phone, and it appeared like he was just talking into air. Lance was always amazed by how the person on the other end could actually hear him.

"Lance?" *Shit*. It was Bruce.

"Is Lance there?" Bruce said.

Lance rolled his eyes. "Yeah, Bruce, this is Lance."

"Lance, hey listen, I was thinking about those data sheets..."

Lance listened to him drone on about it, cursing himself for answering the phone to begin with. He was, after all, sitting on the shitter for God's sake.

Outside, there was an announcement over the PA system but Lance barely registered this as he alternately gave his attention to Bruce's droning and to the new bout of roiling diarrhea that had reared its ugly head again. Lance imagined himself saying to Bruce, "Hey pal, I think I found those data sheets," and then placing the phone next to his ass as he took yet another monstrous shit.

It was really tempting.

Bruce seemed to talk forever. It occurred to Lance that maybe the guy was just lonely. How else could anyone explain volunteering to work over a holiday weekend? As far as Lance knew, Bruce had no special or emergency project with a deadline that would require such a sacrifice. The guy was just a lonely, king shit brown noser. While sitting on the throne listening to Bruce drone on and on, Lance suddenly had a memory jog and the proverbial lightbulb came on.

A name change.

The company generating the bulk of the data sheets was bought out and had to change its name.

"Hey, Bruce, wait a minute," said Lance. "Go look in Vernie's files. I doubt that they are in his computer, but I think that he may have hard copies in his office...right...in the file cabinet under ANGEL FIRE, *not* FIRELINK. I think the name changed and that might be the reason why we could not find them."

Lance had also forgotten about old packrat Vernie. If anyone would have them in hard copy, Vernie would.

Come on Vernie, don't let me down, pardner.

Lance thought that he had detected the slightest amount of disappointment in Bruce's voice as he considered that the mystery might finally be solved. This pettiness dissolved the small amount of sympathy Lance had held in reserve based on the loneliness factor. Lance wedged the phone between his shoulder and his ear as he got some industrial strength sandpaper that masqueraded as toilet paper.

"Okay, Bruce, I'll see ya Monday. Have a good Fourth."

Lance reached around with his right hand, grabbed the phone off his shoulder, and looked at it to make sure that he pushed the END button so that the damned thing would actually disconnect from the other line when he observed with a high degree of disgust that there was a thin film of brown and slippery diarrhea juice *on his hand* and that he had actually smeared some on the END button of his phone.

"Gahhhhh!" Lance hissed as he dropped the phone on the hard tiled floor.

The phone landed hard. Lance watched in despair as the back plate broke off and bounced about five feet away from the face plate, skidding along the smooth tiled floor and coming to a rest near the sink bank. Lance then did something that he had not done all day (well, except when Carl told him the jokes).

He smiled.

Then he began to laugh softly at himself and all the shit (literally) that he had been through today.

At least there was no one else around to see that

Lance thought, thankful for that small bit of grace. Still chuckling, Lance used about half of the roll of toilet paper to clean himself up good and proper. He then pulled up his shorts, buckled his belt, and picked up the pieces of the phone. They fit back together correctly, at least.

He cleaned off the phone thoroughly and then spent a good portion of time washing his hands. He made sure that he splashed a prodigious amount of soap on them, rubbed them vigorously, and then washed them off for a long time under the warm water from the faucet. As he dried his hands with several paper towels from the dispenser, he looked at himself in the mirror, wondering if his week would get any better.

He threw away the paper towels, rubbed his face with his extraordinarily clean hands, and pushed open the men's room door.

CHAPTER FIFTEEN

Assistant Manger Randy Philpot pulled out of the parking lot behind the girls.

They had all been eager to get off work as soon as possible. After they had locked everything down, they had walked to the back, punched out on the automated time clock near the coffee machine, and filed out of the building through the back door. They had all parked in the employee section in the back parking lot. This lot was accessible to a very busy street running behind the store, which meant that they did not even have to drive past the front at all.

None of them noticed Lance's car.

Nor would they have given it a second thought if they had. The outer region of the parking lot was a kind of no man's land. There were several restaurants adjacent to it and it was common for customers to use the *Emporium's* parking lot. The outer part of the lot was also used frequently by teenagers to gather to drink and smoke.

As Randy exited the back parking lot and headed for home, there were in fact three other cars around Lance's grey Mercury Marquis as well as a group of teenagers hanging out, leaning on the hoods, smoking and drinking *Busch* beer that they kept in an ice chest in one of their trunks (Randy suspected that they had some reefers with them as well).

None of them paid any attention to *The Builder's Emporium.*

CHAPTER SIXTEEN

Lance walked out of the men's room and made it about three steps toward the garden hoses when he stopped, sensing that something was not right.

There were no sounds. None at all.

The store was too quiet. Too still. There seemed to be no activity at all. Lance was curious why there were no background noises in the store; no bustling carts with wobbly wheels, no clattering customers, no crying kids, no incomprehensible announcements over the store's public address system. Lance stood motionless and listened.

Nothing.

It was not only unnaturally quiet in *The Builder's*

Emporium, but Lance noticed also that the lighting had changed as well. *Shifted* in some way. It was not dark exactly, but the lighting had definitely changed. Somehow it had become more *dim*. It was as if the store people had turned on the night lights.

They had closed it up.

As Lance stood there, still and silent, he smiled a wry smile while at the same time shaking his head slowly back and forth. Lance came to the realization that, while he had been having his moment in the head, the store had closed. The people had left. They had closed up shop.

And he was still inside.

Unbelievable.

Margie would not believe this. *But, hey there, sport, Margie doesn't really need to know, does she?*

No. Indeed she did not. He thought he would keep this little fact to himself. *Yeah, pal, just mosey on up to the front, make a phone call, whatever. The place is creepy like this. Just make sure that you...*

There was a sound to his right.

Lance realized that he had been holding his breath. Slowly, he turned his head toward the direction of the sound. He listened.

There it was again.

Footfalls.

Soft footfalls, moving slowly. Lance began to feel uneasy. There was really no reason why he *should* feel uneasy.

But he did. He was in a public place, after all. It was not like he was standing in the middle of a cemetery on Halloween night.

Hey, pal, in case you haven't noticed, this place don't look so public at the moment. They shut her down. Probably locked everything up. Locked everything up nice and tight. Sure they did.

Then what made that sound?

He had no immediate answer. Not that he needed one. The store was gigantic. A creation of corporate America that was so huge that it required constant attention. Even if all the day workers went home, a store this size surely would have a night maintenance crew. Lance doubted that the *Emporium* was ever truly empty. There was no way he could be in here alone.

He heard the faint sound of the footfalls again. He definitely was not alone. Nor was he scared, mind you. Shit no. Just a little inquisitive. Just a little *curious* as to why someone would be trying to...*sneak up* on him in a deserted store.

It was odd.

Why would someone be walking toward him without wanting to be heard? At least, that is what it sounded like.

Lance's haggard body was now on full alert. His heart sped up just a little bit, seeming to beat a little heavier in his chest. A distant (and not unpleasant) numbness invaded his arms and legs as a jolt of adrenaline spread the message of alarm. Unable to control the fight or flight reflex of his body,

Lance's beleaguered balls once again wrapped themselves tightly within his nut sac and headed for the safety of his lower belly. For the first time in a very long time, Lance was unconsciously preparing himself for a physical confrontation.

Not that he thought that he would *actually* become involved in a physical confrontation. That was *nuts*. But still, it never hurt to be prepared for these things.

Just in case.

Lance glanced at the sign attached to the end of the aisle where he was standing. The sign was large and had four lines of text: GARDENING, HOSES, LAWN SUPPLIES, RAKES/SHOVELS. Below the sign, at eye level, Lance noticed for the first time a smaller sign that announced: THIS AISLE MAINTAINED BY_____. The sign was a pre-printed form and the name "GREG" had been handwritten in the blank space in large, block letters with a black magic marker.

Lance was standing in GREG's aisle. He wished GREG were here now, pimply faced, decked out in a bright red *Builder's Emporium* vest with complimentary name tag, eager to please–and, *oh yeah*, holding a fucking key to the front door. Yeah, if GREG were here, *he* would definitely know what to do.

Lance placed his body behind the corner of the aisle, at the end just below the signs. The sneaky footfalls had stopped.

Well, two could play at that game.

Lance crouched down, giving his body cover behind the aisle, and peeked his head around the corner to see who was walking softly toward him two aisles down.   As Lance crouched into place

HISSSSSSSSSSSSSSSSSSSSSSSSSSSSSSSSS!!!

there was an ear-splitting hissing sound that shattered the silence of the store.

Lance nearly jumped out of his skin.

He gasped at the noise, shocked and surprised, heart pumping in earnest now, muscles tensed. Lance recognized the sound. It was the loud hissing sound of a large air compressor. There was another hellish hiss as high speed air again escaped from somewhere, two aisles down.

Lance marveled at the situation. Someone had just fired up an air compressor and connected the high speed air hose to something.

Large air compressors were, of course, in stock at *The Builder's Emporium*. Lance recalled seeing them. They were lined up like barrel-chested soldiers along a display line, secured to sturdy wooden pallets and ready for inspection.

About two aisles down.

The huge canisters stood between four and six feet tall and were painted red and tan, depending upon whether you were looking at a "Husky" brand or the "Ingersoll-Rand." Lance could not recall whether they operated on fuel or electricity. But still. He could not fathom why a store employee would crank one up.

What the fu...

Lance's thoughts were cut short when he saw a man come walking around the corner of the aisle, two rows down, about thirty feet from where Lance was, well... *hiding*. The man was smiling and cradled a large tool of some sort that was connected to a hose that trailed behind him and snaked its way around the corner and out of sight in the direction of the noisy compressor.

Lance felt a flush of embarrassment. There he was, *hiding* for Christ's sake, inside *The Builder's Emporium*. He relaxed, took a step toward the main aisle, and began walking toward the man who had appeared. Some store employee (maybe even GREG himself!) who had to stay behind and do some shit work over the holiday. That was truly a bummer. Bad luck old sport. But Lance felt elated that his predicament would soon be resolved.

Lance relaxed, affixed his best "aw shucks" grin on his face, and walked toward the employee.

"Hey, man, I think there's been some mistake, I just need to pick up some stuff and get out. I didn't mean to keep you late on the holiday and all..." Lance said before trailing off.

As he got closer to the man, Lance realized that it definitely was not GREG. There was no red vest, no name tag, and no hint that the man was eager to make a sale or to take care of the customer.

Lance had been walking toward the man and, as he approached, he realized that the man was not smiling. Not exactly. He was grinning in a malicious way that made Lance tense once more, this time for real. The man was *leering*. And his eyes. They were bulging, about to pop out of his skull. Lance stopped in his tracks, still a good distance from the man, and recognized pretty clearly that the guy was not right in the head. The bulging eyes and huge grin were set in front of a large, clean-shaven head.

Lance suddenly wished that he had never gotten off the shitter.

Lance's immediate perception was that the man walking toward him was *rabid*.

Lance thought back to the time that he had actually seen a rabid thing. It had happened during his childhood. He must have been about ten or so, but he remembered it vividly. His family had settled into a farmhouse about two miles outside of a small town in Oklahoma. Although they lived on an acreage with a two lane highway running along the front of the house, they could technically have been characterized as living in the country. Lance had two good-sized dogs, Blackie and Lucky Sam. One afternoon, ten-year-old Lance was outside filling up the food and water dishes for the dogs when he heard them both growling. Lance looked around and saw a skunk ambling its way toward the food dishes.

Toward *him*.

As the skunk waddled toward him and the dogs, Lance was afraid that the dogs would attack it and get sprayed. It would be weeks before that damned polecat smell would come out of their coats and, as the dogs charged, Lance was afraid that the skunk might hurt the dogs. At the time, he had no idea if skunks had some other defense besides the stink spray.

But when the dogs took off after the skunk, a curious thing happened.

After initially charging, both dogs backed away as they approached it. Blackie actually whined and ran around behind Lance, while Lucky Sam stood his ground growling deep in his chest but not attacking. Lance was amazed that such a small critter could win a standoff with the dogs. He could see that the dogs had not been sprayed, yet they seemed scared.

In fact, the skunk appeared not to have noticed the dogs at all. It continued to trundle along toward the food dishes, seemingly oblivious to the two dogs and to Lance. As it trudged closer, Lance backed away a few feet, but still remained close, intrigued by the little critter. As the skunk approached the food, Lance could see that the animal was sick. Its mouth hung open and it drooled along the sides. Its fur was a matted mess that seemed to be caked with mud and shit along its hindquarters. It looked directly up at Lance just before it got to the food dishes, and then just appeared to lose interest in Lance as it proceeded to eat.

Monsieur rabid skunk was Lance's one and only experience with a rabid animal.

Until now.

The countenance of the man standing in front of him gave Lance the same sickening feeling as that rabid skunk had all those years ago.

With the skunk, Lance's mother had come out of the house to see what was going on when she had heard Lucky Sam growling. She had recognized the danger immediately and ordered Lance into the house. Lance did not go inside the house, but rather watched from the back porch as the skunk continued to eat from the dog bowls.

Lance's mother had called the local police who proceeded to give her some bullshit excuse about the house being technically outside the city limits. They had refused to come out. The Garfield County Sheriff's Office was located in the county seat about twenty minutes away and there was no way they were coming out on a call like that. In the end, his mother had gone into the bedroom, loaded the old bolt action .22 that had been her grandfather's, and had shot the poor animal as it ate the dog food.

Lance felt that he would very much like to have a bolt action .22 at this moment. The man was clearly not a store employee and was definitely crazy as a shithouse rat.

"Phoebe." The man whispered, shaking his head slowly from side to side. "Thought I would forget? Did you really think that?"

Lance had no response to this.

Phoebe?

Lance's mouth had gone dry. He tried to reply but only a small, unintelligible croak came out of his mouth. He cleared his throat and spoke slowly.

"My name is not Phoebe and I think that I need to leave now."

But Lance did not move. Although the man's bizarre appearance and statements made Lance feel uneasy (on guard, you might say), his initial fright was now working in the background of his mind. His primary emotion at the present was in the neighborhood of cautious curiosity because the situation was just so bizarre.

Lance sized up the man's physical dimensions. He was about the same height as Lance, but much more muscular in the upper body. The man's face was framed by sharp, angular lines, with a square jaw that housed big, block teeth.

But the thing that caught Lance's attention was the heavy tool the man cradled in his hands. It hung low across the man's hips. To Lance, it looked like a giant zip gun, but it wasn't.

It was in fact a *Senco 650 FramePro Pneumatic Nail Gun.*

The *Senco* weighed 8.4 pounds, had a rubber hand-grip for *comfort*, and shot out nails at 120psi. The business end of it was pointed at Lance.

He stood there frozen, unable to comprehend what was happening.

In the distance, one of the big air compressors hissed loudly again and, at that instant, Lance heard a buzzing sound by his right ear. It sounded like a huge mosquito flying past his ear.

Then another.

Pphhhhttttt

Even when Lance finally realized that the man was *shooting* nails at him, he still could not move.

As the third nail whizzed past Lance's head, the primal part of his brain pushed the bright red panic button in his subconscious and took over. It was in charge of survival and recognized immediately what his civilized mind had not, which was of course that the crazy fuck was shooting large, long nails at his *face*.

Aiming at my face!

Lance backed up and was just about to make a break for the front door when he felt a sharp bolt of pain in his left hand.

"*Ahhhhhhhh!*"

It felt like a vice had clamped down on his middle finger (his fuckfinger as Chet liked to say), or perhaps like he was getting stung there by a three-pound wasp. He tried to pull his hand up to his face for inspection but it was held fast in place, actually *stuck* by a nail to the stack of two-by-fours in front of which he had been standing.

Lance looked down at his hand, dimly aware that more projectiles were zipping past his head, and saw that the top of the last joint of the middle finger on his left hand was pinned to the wood by a *nail*.

A big one.

As he looked at his agonized finger, he saw another nail *stick* in the wood inches from his hand.

"HOW DOES *THAT* FEEL?!" the man roared at Lance, who by this time had wandered into fear's neighborhood and was very close to full tilt panic. Lance could hear the *phhhhttt* sound as the gun air-jettisoned the nails toward him. He also saw that the man was shaking with rage which seemed to affect his aim.

"I'VE GOT A LITTLE STINGER MYSELF!" said the man thickly.

Lance felt another nail hit his leg, this one sinking like a dart into the fleshy part of his outer right calf before being carried by inertia and sailing through the skin and out again like a vicious kebab skewer, the head of the nail catching flesh and pulling on it as it exited and skidded along the floor.

The primal part of Lance's brain had been screaming *RED ALERT!*

for several seconds and now the civilized Lance was on board as well. Shaking his head slowly back and forth in the way that people do when they can not believe what they are seeing, Lance recognized that if he stayed there the lunatic was going to shoot him full of nails.

He had to get away, and quickly.

Despite the pain in his finger, and now a new spray of pain in his leg, Lance reached around to try and pull out the nail but immediately felt that it was not going to budge. He then did the only thing he could do, which was to pull his finger away from the nail on which it was impaled.

He clenched his jaws together, knotted muscle and

tendon bulging on either side of his face, and made a low growling sound as he tried to yank his hand free. His finger slid down the smooth shaft of the nail toward the large, round head. It stuck there for a moment. With a huge grunt and with his teeth grinding together, Lance pulled his finger off the nail. As he pulled, the head of the nail ripped an even larger ragged hole through the tip of his finger.

The pain was exquisite.

Lance wrapped his right hand around his agonized left-hand finger, squeezing tight to stem the bleeding and to stop the pain. At the same time, he made a quick dash to the front of the store, yelling, "I'M NOT PHOEBE YOU CRAZY FUCK!" as he ran.

The man made no apparent attempt to run after him.

As he ran, Lance glanced back and noticed that something about the air hose fitted to the butt of the nail gun had distracted the man momentarily.

Cradling his shredded finger–and registering pain in his right calf–Lance bolted past the checkout counters and headed for the large glass doors of the front entrance. In his panic-stricken mind, he had planned to simply go running out the huge sliding glass doors. Hell, he would not even have to touch them. All he would have to do is stand before them, break the invisible beam, and they would just slide open automatically.

That was his plan.

Running past the bank of checkout stands, Lance slowed as he assessed the bad news that lay before him. He stood still, shaking his head as he stared at the entrance to the store, the very spot where he had walked *in* less than an hour ago. Holding his finger, now feeling it throb with each beat of his heart, he saw that not only were the glass doors *not* going to slide open he could not even break through the glass to get out.

Security doors.

Lance saw that his way out was blocked by an overhead metal sliding door that had been rolled down over the glass doors. It was a formidable security precaution Lance was sure, but it was

mighty fucking inconvenient when one was, say, being chased by a crazy fuck with a nail gun

"Are you *shitting* me?" Lance said to himself. He wanted to scream in frustration, but had the presence of mind to make as little noise as possible.

He stood there, breathing heavily through his mouth. He looked down at his leg where he had been hit with the second nail. He could see blood running down his calf from the through-and-through holes that had been ripped through his flesh, but not as much as he would have thought; nor was the pain nearly as bad as the pain in his finger, although it *did* hurt every time he took a step.

"Fuck *me*," Lance whimpered, trying to think of what to do next.

As Lance stood frozen with indecision, he heard the man approaching. He turned around and saw that the man was holding something in his hands. Lance thought at first that it was an axe, but upon much-to-close-for-comfort inspection he saw that the object had a blunt steel head opposite the blade. It looked like a cross between and axe and a sledgehammer.

A *maul*.

The man was holding an eight pound Black Knight maul. It appeared to Lance as a crude, medieval weapon.

A maul! How could this possibly be happening?

Lance's mind reeled.

The man held the maul like he intended to use it, right hand choked up near the head, left hand slid down near the bottom of the long wooden handle.

As he advanced, Lance bolted again, still squeezing his throbbing finger and taking note of his injured right calf. He ran down the main aisle and could hear the man in pursuit. Lance was hyped up on adrenaline and outpaced the crazy bastard who ran behind him still holding the maul.

After running a good distance and no longer hearing the man in pursuit, Lance stopped and turned around, trying to clear his head and take stock of the situation.

He saw that the lunatic was still approaching, but walking now, not running. Walking with *purpose* in his stride which made him more frightening. Lance realized that the man was in no hurry to do what he intended to do. He was taking his time.

Lance looked around and tried to think. He was standing next to a large display in the center of the main aisle. He glanced down and saw that it was a large round plastic tub filled with octagonal nuts. Big, heavy ones, about the size of half dollars. Lance had no idea what they could be used for in the normal course of things.

Lance grabbed one in his right hand, felt its weight, and then rocked back and threw it as hard as he could, trying to hit the advancing man between his bugged-out eyes. The metal projectile sailed through the air and, amazingly, hit the man in the side of the head with a sickening thud, although it looked like the man had moved his head at the last minute and the nut only glanced off his head at a harmless angle.

Grazed him, only grazed him, shit, I needed a head shot

Lance felt that he had just crossed a threshold of sorts. He had never thrown such an object in anger at another human being, and certainly had never intended to inflict major injuries to another person in a conflict. But he found himself intending these things now and the realization made him ill.

Why didn't the man just *stop*?

Although Lance was still terrified, there was a new emotion making its presence known in his mind. It had been percolating around in Lance's jumbled thoughts, flitting in and out of his consciousness during the last few minutes, and now made its grand entrance. Lance felt a refreshing jolt of *anger* plunging its way headlong into *fury*. This crazy fuck meant to hurt him, possibly *kill* him.

In fact, Lance had felt a muted sense of triumph when his missile–the giant nut–hit the man in the head. But that feeling had been short-lived. Although Lance could now see what looked like a thin trickle of blood making its way down the side of the man's face, the man seemed to shake off the hit and now smiled again while continuing to advance, not losing his grip on the maul.

"OHHHHH...YOU SHOULD NOT HAVE DONE THAT," said the man as he wiped the blood off his cheek with the back of his hand.

Lance grabbed another one of the heavy nuts and chunked it at the man, harder this time. It sailed wildly to the right and the man did not even slow down this time. Lance reached for another nut, raised it, hesitated, and then dropped it back into the display bin.

No good. Lance could tell that his attack was no good.

He had gotten lucky with the first nut but could not try to hit the man again, at least until the man was close enough to kill him with the maul. No, this was no good. He had to find a better weapon or take flight.

Flight

Lance backed up a few more steps, placing the large bin of oversized nuts between him and the man. Lance was near the wall now. He looked up and saw a huge banner hanging from the ceiling, proclaiming in large white letters against a bright red background: LUMBER.

At the end of the aisle closest to the wall was a huge circular saw mounted on a vertical stand. Over it hung another large banner, christening it the "CUTTING CENTER."

Further down, on the last aisle, was a large area which displayed huge stacks of lumber and plywood.

Lance looked at the items displayed in the aisle to his left. General tools: chisels, screwdrivers, socket sets, mounted and handheld circular saws, and small, single blade hatchets.

The display item closest to Lance was a large collection of the actual blades that fit the circular saws. Rows of them. They were heavy, metal discs with extremely sharp, serrated teeth. Blades of all kinds, shapes and sizes. Mostly for wood, but a few for metal and concrete. One line of blades was for use strictly on "ferrous materials."

Lance's first choice on this aisle, which was maintained in tidy fashion by CARL according to the sign announcing such things, was the large selection of handheld hatchets, ideal for camping, cutting down small trees and, apparently, self-defense and hand-to-hand combat.

But the hatchets were too far down the aisle.

Although the man was advancing slowly, he was still moving quickly enough. Lance looked again at the maul that the man held in his hands. A hatchet would be no good. Even if he was able to grab a hatchet, he would be the proverbial idiot who decided to take a knife to a gun fight.

Still keeping his eye on the man, Lance reached out and grabbed one of the saw blades. He winced as he pulled it from the display. The teeth of the blades were very sharp, and the metal was dense and very heavy. He felt the steel dig into the skin of his fingers as he held the blade, but did not feel that he had been cut.

Lance had in fact selected a sixteen tooth Oldham (*since 1857!*) general purpose, industrial carbide circular saw blade. He grabbed the blade carefully between his right index finger and his thumb, reading the descriptive label

extra fast ripping and crosscutting!

as he heaved it overhanded as hard as he could. Lance let out a whimper as he did it. At the height of the throw, just when he stopped the backward windup with forward energy, the sharp teeth of the steel blade sliced through the skin of his thumb and forefinger.

"Shit!" Lance squealed as he flung the blade. He immediately brought his thumb to his mouth and ran his tongue along the deep cut there, grimacing at the warm metallic taste of his own blood.

At the top of Lance's windup to throw the circular saw blade, the man had stopped in his tracks. With his thumb in his mouth like an infant, Lance watched as the whirring blade sliced through the air, traveling very fast and on target toward the man's head.

At the last second, just before the sharp steel teeth were about to embed themselves in the soft tissue of the man's nose, the man simply raised the steel head of the maul about one foot, holding it defensively in front of his face. The flying blade struck the head of the maul dead solid, steel on steel, emitting a solid metallic *ping!*

After striking the head of the maul, the saw blade, with three teeth bent obscenely backwards, simply bounced back a few feet and fell to the concrete floor with a clang.

The man lowered the maul. Then he smiled at Lance.

"Gonna give you something to squeal *about*," said the man.

He was very close now, and coming at Lance faster than before. Lance looked quickly at the blades and, further down, at the hatchets, feeling the searing pain in both hands now, at the nail wound on his left finger and the new deep cut on his right thumb and forefinger. The surge of anger that had prompted his flurry of activity was dissipating.

He suddenly felt stupid and weak.

Needed gloves to handle those saw blades. Damn, how could I be so stupid? Throwing saw blades and nuts?

He had to flee. It was either that or fight this man while unarmed and injured. But where could he run?

Lance looked back at the man. He was grinning again and advancing quickly now, the blood running down his face making him look even more maniacal. Lance realized with despair that he had not inflicted any serious injuries at all. From the looks of things, he had, in fact, succeeded only in angering the man. Lance stood there facing down the man like an inexperienced matador who, having injured the bull, was hesitant about what to do next.

In a split-second decision, Lance turned on his heels and took off running down the main aisle. In two steps he was in a full sprint, both arms pistoning up and down, the shredded finger of his left hand and the sliced thumb of his right slinging droplets of blood with every swing of his arms.

He had no idea where he was going.

CHAPTER SEVENTEEN

Lance slowed as he rounded the corner. He glanced back to see if the man was still pursuing him. He was not. Lance stopped and tried to listen for sounds. Sweat beaded on his forehead and he could feel the beat of his heart as it throbbed in the tips of his injured fingers. All the nerve endings in his fingers cried in unison.

We're here, buddy! All pain generators present and accounted for!

Lance was so hyped up, it was difficult to hear. The blood pumped fiercely through his head and seemed to interfere with the work that his ears were trying to do. His breath came in huge gasps, chest heaving as if he had just ran two miles rather than fifty feet.

No sounds.

If the man was not chasing him then he had turned around and doubled back to intercept Lance at the corner. Lance took an involuntary step backwards.

Or, dear Watson, the crazy fuck wants me to think that he has doubled back so that I will turn around and double back right into him, or maybe–hah, hah, here's a good one–maybe he thinks that I will think that he would think to double back...

Lance was paralyzed with indecision.

He was on the defensive. Vulnerable. He did not like the feeling. But which way to go? He saw no readily available weapons in this aisle. At least none that could counter an attack from a *maul*.

He had to find an exit.

The front was not a viable option. Although there were phones there, he doubted he could keep the maniac at bay long enough to make a phone call. He had no idea if the back of the store was locked down as well. Lance figured that it probably was, but it seemed like the only option at this point.

Other than, say, a fight to the death with Phoebe's secret admirer using gardening tools. Jesus. How could this be happening?

Lance wiped the sweat from his forehead. He was on the verge of panic. He dared not run back the way he came; yet, he was afraid to continue further down the main aisle. If the man *was* waiting in ambush, Lance would have no chance.

If only he knew where the entrance to the back of the store was located. He was pretty sure that it was by the men's room, but he had not been paying attention when he had been back there shitting his guts out. It was not a priority at the time, but it sure was now. If only he could see the layout of the store.

Up

Even as the word popped into his head, Lance tilted his head and looked up. He saw that lumber lined the aisle, stacked up nearly thirty feet. The stacks of lumber, four-by-eight sheets of plywood, eight foot two-by-fours and large boards, were supported by steel beams which looked like sections of railroad track. The weight of the lumber had to be enormous, but the steel support beams looked equal to the task.

It appeared to Lance that if he could make it to the top of the lumber stacks, he should be able to see the layout of the store's interior, not to mention being able to track the psycho who was trying to kill him.

Lance began to climb.

CHAPTER EIGHTEEN

Walter waited.

He had made his way to this place but now could not remember why he had done so. The grids provided no guidance or answers. They were black.

His head ached. It was difficult for him to conceptualize the cause of his pain, but at that moment he had a sense that he had been *stung* by something. The creature in the store with him first appeared as a man when it had come out of the men's room. Walter had thought that maybe one of the checkout girls was the cause of his pain.

He had been thinking that, and trying to formulate a plan to deal with it, when he had seen the man standing near the garden hoses *change* into something that was not human. The form changed again into an emotion of hate that he identified with Phoebe who had caused him and his mother so much pain and sorrow, and then again into a giant monster with a scorpion tail (*Frankie?*).

He was no longer sure what it was, but he *was* sure that if he destroyed it, the pain in his temples would go away. The pain was already spreading. His left arm was tingling and was on the verge of perhaps going numb. Walter's perception warped as he stood in the aisle trying to clear his head. He sensed that the link between the creature and the pain in his head could be broken if he destroyed the creature.

One thing was for sure. He had seen *fear* in the creature's eyes as it ran down the aisle. This was good. Walter viewed it as confirmation. If it was afraid, that meant it knew what it had coming.

Walter had situated himself down the aisle, expecting it to run past him by now, but so far there was no sign of it. He could not hear it either. It was up to something.

Was it there at all? He did not know.

If it was, it was not going to run straight into his ambush. Walter was patient; he knew he would get it soon enough.

As he waited, Walter's mind degenerated further as the tumor fed on his brain. Over the course of many years, he had segregated his feelings of fear and shame into a construct that he associated with (and sometimes called by name) Phoebe. In the dim logic of his mind, he was sure that if he could destroy it then the agonizing jumble of emotions and thoughts that sat tangled in his head would loosen and he would be free.

He had tried to destroy it once before in this place. He *thought* that he had succeeded, but the police officers had taken him away before he could be sure. Now, he had come back to make sure, to make positively *certain*, once and for all, that thing causing him so much pain was destroyed.

He hefted the maul.

The thing was playing games again. If it would not come to him, then Walter would have to go to it.

He heard a sound.

So it was not that far away. But not coming his way, either. It was up to something. Something *evil*. Walter took a slugger's stance with the maul and proceeded to take a step toward the noise.

CHAPTER NINETEEN

Lance had been making good progress scaling the lumber piles. The boards were stacked on the shelves perpendicular to the shelving supports, which meant that the ends of the boards faced Lance and extended out away from him. If all the boards had been pressed flush with the others in the stack, it would have been difficult to scale them; but some of the boards stuck out and made excellent handholds.

The problem Lance encountered was the steel beam supporting the stacks was slick. Climbing up, he had to use it to support his weight as he made it from one stack to the other. He was about ten feet up, holding onto the edges of two boards, when the rubber sole of his sneaker slipped off the steel support beam with an audible slipping sound and, because his body weight was now supported only by his arms, he hung suspended in the air, swinging back and forth, making furtive sounds as he gasped for air and willed his hands and arms to support the weight of his body.

It had been a very long time since he had supported his entire body weight with his arms only. It was much more arduous than he had imagined it would be. He swung back and forth, trying to gain purchase onto the steel support beam with his feet. This slip had caused him to panic. If the crazy man was close by then he surely would have heard Lance trying to climb.

Lance felt *vulnerable*.

He scrambled faster, sensing danger close by. He tried to climb up quickly to the top of the second stack of lumber and out of danger. Almost there.

If only he could get to the top and think–

Lance sensed rather than heard the man's attack.

He instinctively lifted his legs, bringing his knees up to his chest as he hung by his hands from the two-by-fours above. He looked down in time to see the maul drive into the wood pile right where his left foot had been a split-second before.

That would have taken off my foot, that would have...

The man was growling now, working frantically to work the sharp edge of the maul out of the board into which it was embedded.

Lance stared down at the man trying to free the maul. The swing was incredibly powerful and it looked as if the blade had sunk in all the way. The man stopped, sensing that the maul was too stuck to pull out. He looked up at Lance and their eyes locked. A wave of terror washed over Lance as he stared into the madness he saw there.

There was no sanity there.

No humanity. No hint that Lance could offer to discuss the situation rationally, maybe even offer some sort of compromise or truce. Lance saw the eyes of a predator and, renewed with yet another jolt of adrenaline, he pulled himself up and over the top stack of two-by-fours, landing flat on his face against the cool wood. Even with the strength fueled by fear, his arms began to ache from the effort. He realized just how out of shape he had become.

But still he could not rest.

Lance got to his knees and peered over the side. The man was climbing up after him and moving fast. Lance saw that he was climbing up the stacks using the embedded maul as a handhold, and then a foothold as he climbed. Lance looked around and weighed his options, trying not to panic. He was sure of one thing, and that was if the man made it up to where Lance was it would end badly. He could not win a hand-to-hand fight with this man.

Lance had an excellent view of the back of the store. He also noticed that he could run lengthways down the top of the aisle toward the front of the store, stepping on the lumber stacks as he went toward the checkout counters. He would have to hop from stack to stack, but it looked doable.

But then what?

There was no exit that way. And he had no weapons up here.

Panic

Lance turned back to the advancing madman. He could see the muscles ripple in the arms that carried the man upward, see the tendons in the forearms that flexed and strained with the effort. All of a sudden running was out of the question. This man would catch him.

Lance looked down at his own feet and intuitively grasped his powerful positional advantage. He took a step back, bent down, and picked up one of the loose eight-foot-long two-by-fours upon which he stood. Using it like a long, thick spear, but with no point, Lance stepped to the edge and prepared for a confrontation.

The man was swinging up on the last beam, just below Lance's feet. Lance poised himself to strike. He took aim at the man's head and, just as the man looked up for his final ascent, Lance sent the blunt end of the board hurtling toward the man's face. The man looked up just in time to see the board zipping down from above.

Lance felt primordial glee as the edge of the board hit the man's cheek with a sickening thud. The edge of the heavy board, driven downward with surprising force by gravity and Lance's energized muscles, cut through the skin covering the man's cheekbone and, as Lance observed in horror, a large flap of skin on the man's face peeled away as the board continued its path downward. The board continued its trajectory downward and slipped off the man's face, falling with a clatter to the cement floor below, one end gleaming with warm, red blood.

To Lance's astonishment, the man actually hung on for a few seconds after being struck by the board. Rather than pick up another board for a second attack, Lance looked down at the man, trying again to comprehend what motivated his actions. He saw that a flap of skin about the size of a large band-aid hung down under the man's right eye. The man blinked for a few seconds–unable to focus–and then released his handhold and dropped to the floor below.

As the man landed on the floor, his left foot landed awkwardly on the edge of the board that had caused the damage to his face. The man's ankle buckled and he fell backward, hands splayed out to his sides to break his fall.

Lance reacted to this prime opportunity and turned to pick up another board. He grasped another of the long boards and swung it around so that he held it vertically clasped in both hands. He stepped carefully to the edge again, hoping that the man was still splayed out on the floor so that he could get a clean shot again. Maybe another clean *head* shot.

But as he looked down the man was gone.

CHAPTER TWENTY

Tommy Jones was scared.

He left Harmon's office with the very unpleasant feeling that Harmon suspected something. Tommy knew that he had fucked up in a major way by being lax with Walter. By not following *procedure*. The ass-chewing he had just received from Harmon was well deserved, but at least he came away from it with the feeling that his job was still safe.

But he had seen something in Harmon's eyes that told him that Harmon suspected something. Suspecting was one thing, proving was another. Tommy had been careful over the years in concealing Walter's...*gratuities*.

For one thing, he never took *too* much. When he had been on the force–the *real* police force and not this bubblegum shit detail in the nuthouse that he had been doing for the last five years–one of the old officers had taken Tommy under his wing.

Tommy recalled those many years ago, as they stood there in the drug house, just the two of them, looking at each other and then back to the huge pile of cash on the table, and then back to each other again. They had eventually reached an understanding, in the process of which Tommy had received a life lesson that had served him well. One that he had never forgotten.

Tommy had followed the lead of the older officer and they each had pocketed several thousand dollars worth of the crumpled bills. When Tommy had reached for the rest of it, his partner had shaken his head.

No.

Tommy had said nothing at the time, but had raised his eyebrow, questioning the old man.

Why not?

There was no one else around and there must have been over thirty-thousand dollars on the table. Tommy had seen absolutely no reason to leave any of it. In fact, he had been a little bit pissed off at the prospect of taking only a few thousand when the mother lode had been sitting there for the taking. But the older man had just shaken his head again, this time more forcefully. They had reached an impasse.

"Listen to me, son," said his partner, "and listen real close." He then looked directly at Tommy and said, very slowly: "Pigs get fat. *Hogs get slaughtered.*"

At the time, Tommy had not been convinced and, although he had gotten the general drift of it, he had thought that it was foolishness to just leave it. But in the end he had deferred to the old man's judgment and took no more.

As the prosecution of the case had progressed, the defendants had asserted that they were the victims of dirty cops. But the allegations never stuck. At this particular drug scene, the narcs who had conducted surveillance on the house and had investigated the drug dealers had known that there was money in the house.

They had just not known *how much.*

Months later, as Tommy and his partner had waited in the hallway of the courthouse to testify in the case, Tommy understood. If there had been no cash at all in the house, the narcs would know that something was wrong. Red flags would have gone up and, although they may not have said anything directly about it, their written reports would have indicated otherwise, and would have made for interesting reading by the prosecutor and the defense lawyers. Tommy had understood that the old man had been right. There just had to be *some* money there.

There just had to be *enough.*

Pigs get fat; hogs get slaughtered.

Never take too much.

Over the years, Tommy had developed his own set of rules. Never take anything that could be traced. It was very rare that Tommy took anything other than cash from Walter-in fact, he could not recall ever taking anything other than cash-and never in large amounts. It was partly because Walter was restricted on the amount of cash that he could have on hand; but mostly it was because pigs get fat, hogs get slaughtered.

Perhaps the most important lesson that Tommy had learned was that he never did any favors for Walter that could ever cause any serious problems if things went awry. Not that Tommy particularly cared if Walter hurt or even killed someone. The point was that any incidents like that would likely lead back to him.

He did not need that kind of exposure.

And so it went. For years. Walter's requests were modest. He needed books to occupy his mind; occasionally he would want a certain food, maybe a little longer in the shower or on the exercise yard, perhaps a few more phone calls than he was otherwise allowed. Just little things. Innocuous things. And Tommy could name his price, within reason. It was so lucrative that Tommy found himself irritated that Walter had conned the shrink into having him transferred to Jackson. Walter had been one of those cash cows that did not come along very often.

But the lowered security risk level was inexplicable to Tommy. Walter was dangerous; and usually he was thinking one step ahead of everyone else.

But during the last few months, Tommy had noticed that Walter's mental state had been deteriorating. Walter had begun acting even crazier than usual. Then he had started forgetting things. Sometimes he would say things that did not make sense, or respond inappropriately to a question asked.

More to the point for Tommy, old Walter had been a little bit lax on providing the cash that Tommy required in return for the favors. A person of Walter's intelligence should not have had any trouble doing any of those things, yet he had. Tommy did not think it was a ruse, but with Walter one had to explore all possibilities.

If it was up to Tommy, Walter would spend the rest of his life in the Big House. Crazy or not, prison was where he belonged. There was no way Walter should be in Jackson. It was just asking for trouble.

But Tommy was not in charge and it was not his call. The medical transfer had gone through. Tommy's only job had been to transport Walter to Jackson and drop him off at his new digs. *Technically* Walter was at the high security level until they got to Jackson. Once there, Tommy was to take the cuffs off and leave Walter in Jackson without them.

When Walter had wanted to take a smoke break outside before they left, Tommy had thought it was a little bit unusual because Walter did not smoke. But Walter had told him that he used to smoke and wanted one in the clean air before they hit the road. Walter had made it worth his while. Tommy had ended up shaking three Marlboros out of his pack, giving them to

Walter, and then leading him to the side of the motor pool so he could smoke before they left. Tommy had gone inside to get out of the heat and catch the news. He had actually forgotten about Walter by the time he realized that something was wrong.

Tommy thought it best to make a big production out of searching for Walter and going up to his room. He had to look surprised. But that part was easy. He *was* surprised.

Walter had a ticket out of Spring Hill, out of belly-chains and piss-smelling hallways, and into an expensive facility in Jackson with no perimeter. Although there might have been some restrictions, he would have been basically free to come and go as he pleased, not to mention having access to the things Tommy gave him but without having to pay Tommy's full retail price.

Tommy could think of absolutely no reason for Walter to go AWOL and risk all that on the very day he was supposed to be transported. Walking away like that would be considered an escape from custody which meant not only no Jackson, but also even more restricted incarceration at Spring Hill itself. It made no sense to Tommy.

He had stopped *trying* to understand it.

What he *did* understand was that Harmon had a hunch.

Harmon had a hunch that Tommy was up to something under-the-table with Walter. Harmon was a sharp old bastard. Tommy had seen it in Harmon's eyes as he had gone over Tommy's story, detail by detail, stopping at certain places and staring at Tommy as if to say *Really? That's your story?*

In the end, Tommy had not cracked, and Harmon had seemed content with the explanation given, or at least had no evidence that the explanation given was untrue. Tommy had slunk out of Harmon's office like a whipped dog, but he now felt like he would survive it.

But still. He found himself wondering *where* Walter had gone.

As he stood in his apartment taking off his uniform, Tommy Jones had, perhaps for the first time in his life, a pang of guilt over something he had done. The more he thought about it, the more it bothered him. He then realized that his irritation was not caused by guilt; it was caused by the fact that Walter had played him for a sucker. Tommy was embarrassed because he had never seen it coming.

Because it made no fucking sense

Now that crazy fuck was AWOL. Who was to say that he would not come after Tommy? Who knew how crazies thought? Tommy was not particularly concerned, but still. When he thought about it, he had squeezed ol' Walter plenty over the years and payback was definitely a bitch. But the more he thought about it, the less likely it seemed that Walter would come after him. Walter was nuts, but Tommy never got the feeling that he took their relationship personally. It was always just business.

Still, better safe than sorry.

Tommy laid his handgun on the table as he ate a sandwich and a bowl of hot canned soup that tasted surprisingly good. He thought about Walter. What he talked about. What appeared to drive him. He tried to think where Walter might have gone, and why.

A mental image formed in Tommy's mind of him grabbing Walter by the scruff of his neck and hauling him into Harmon's office. Maybe even kicking the back of Walter's legs, forcing him to his knees, showing Harmon that everything was all right. That even though Tommy had fucked up, he had rectified the situation.

Tommy thought of his old partner again. Harmon reminded him a lot of the old bastard. They both had good judgment and knew when to say yes, and more importantly when to say no. One time Tommy had asked his partner for a little help with a problem. His partner had listened as Tommy explained the situation but, to Tommy's surprise, had refused to help. It had ended up being a very good decision on his part.

He had just shaken his head and told Tommy, "Clean up your own mess, son." That was sage advice.

Clean up your own mess.

Tommy finished the bowl of soup and the sandwich while still thinking about how to clean up the mess he had made.

CHAPTER TWENTY-ONE

Lance stood on the wood stacks for a while, breathing hard and holding the board which had become his pitiful weapon, waiting to see if the man would have another go at him. Lance held the board vertically in a position that made him look like a person who had declared himself king of *The Builder's Emporium* and was daring anyone to oppose him. He felt a little bit ridiculous, but that did not stop him from striking the pose.

After a few minutes–*how many? one? five? he could not tell*–with no sign of the man, the tension drained from Lance little by little. He laid the board down as quietly as he could, listening for any sounds that would indicate the man's location.

There were none.

Lance breathed, trying to not make any noise. He felt relatively safe in this location, but still could probably do nothing if the man went to the other end, climbed up, and then came after him over the stacks. He considered this nasty possibility and felt like crying.

God, how long had it been since he had felt like this?

What made it worse was the fact that Lance was fairly certain that he had not injured the man enough for him to call off the attack. He would be back.

That crazy fuck would be back.

While he tried to come to grips with the situation, Lance had a moment of clarity. This ordeal was going to end badly for both of them–*one* of them for sure. All indications were that the man would keep pushing it to a resolution. Maybe one with finality. The man appeared to be too crazed to stop without some serious damage being done to him. Lance did not like the idea that he was going to be pushed that far–to seriously injuring or even killing this man.

Lance quickly inspected all sides of his lumber stack, looking down to make sure that the man was not silently scaling upward. There was no sign of him. Lance sat down cross-legged, something else that he had not done in years, and pondered his options.

He looked around and saw a piece of red cloth nailed to the end of one of the boards. He had seen such rags many times while driving. Truckers displayed them on long cargo to notify drivers following behind that there were long boards sticking out of the back. Lance grabbed the rag, pulled it free of the nail, and wrapped it around his left middle finger, even though the bleeding appeared to have stopped.

It was difficult to do one-handed, particularly with the sliced thumb and forefinger of his right hand. His right calf was singing again, and he was still sick from the bad fish and hungover. He was thirsty, too, and found it difficult to gather his thoughts.

Lance wondered if he was going into shock.

He sat down again on the lumber stack, trying to gather his wits. The rolling waves of diarrhea had ceased. That was one in the win column at least. He thought wryly that he had discovered a cure for the runs.

Got the trots? That ain't nothin' a little fight with a homicidal maniac won't cure.

Above all, Lance still could not believe that this was happening. It seemed like it was just a few minutes before that he had been sitting on the jakes, talking on the phone to Bruce the Deuce, and enjoying the scenery in the men's room.

On the phone with Bruce

Lance felt to his right. It was still there, clipped to his belt. He took the cell phone off its clip and turned it in his right hand so that he could see the face of the phone. He pushed the POWER button and waited.

Nothing.

He waited some more. Sometimes it just took the thing a few seconds to warm up and acquire a signal.

Still nothing.

He pushed the button again, and then a few more times, each time expecting the face to illuminate in the green glow which signaled that communication with the outside world was possible. Lance shook the phone and then hit it a few times against the boards.

Fuck. This was not fair.

Lance wondered just how it was possible that he would drop his cell phone and break it just prior to being *treed* by a homicidal maniac. What were the chances of that happening?

Well, pardner, from the looks of things here, I'd say the chances of that happening are right at 100%

Instead of talking to the police dispatcher, Lance simply clipped the useless phone back in its place out of force of habit and, for the first time in a long time, wept as quietly as he could.

CHAPTER TWENTY-TWO

Margie carried a basket as she walked from the kitchen out to the deep freeze in the garage. She set the basket down on the garage floor as she lifted the lid. Swirls of white mist drifted in the air, partially obscuring her view. She swished the mist away with a wave of her hand and saw that the deep freeze was packed mostly with hot dog packs and pre-made hamburger patties, although there was also a rump roast near the bottom, stacks of frozen pizzas, and two packs of frozen shrimp that had been sitting at the very bottom for over four years.

Margie took out several packs of hot dogs and hamburgers, placing them in the basket before closing the lid and walking back inside. She placed the frozen food in the fridge so that it would be thawed out by tomorrow. She had to make two trips to the deep freeze to get everything.

The hotdogs and burgers were for everyone to cook themselves, or maybe Lance or one of the uncles would man the grill as they usually did, swilling cheap beer and talking sports and who knows what else.

In the kitchen again, she turned her attention to her project: a huge ham that she had bought for the occasion, all twenty-two pounds of it. It was going to be a booger to prepare correctly. Not that she minded. Margie enjoyed cooking. Always had. She had spent all day yesterday making preparations.

Every year around this time, she spent a full two days of wonderful solitude in her kitchen followed by a day of maddening chaos when the rest of the family descended upon her house for the big cook-out and get-together. She enjoyed the quiet before the storm. But, in truth, the storm wasn't so bad either. Although she often chided Lance about his rambunctious family, she was close to them and (another truth be told) she sort of liked being the center of attention during the big family holidays, and the Fourth of July was a big one.

In the childhood home of Marjorie Annette Richardson, the preparation of the family meal was very important, and she still had very warm and vivid memories of when her mother had allowed her to help out in the kitchen. Linda Richardson loved to make a production of it.

Things had to be *just so.*

Margie looked over her kitchen which, like her mother's, was large and full of spices and utensils; mostly cast iron pots and pans and cookbooks. She decided to go ahead and start preparing the ham instead of waiting for Lance to return. She would just make him do the rest of the chores that she would have done if he had gotten back in time. She was a little bit irritated that he was not back already.

She selected one of the cast iron pots, scrubbed it thoroughly with coarse salt, then rinsed it out. Margie then seasoned the pot by rubbing it down with canola oil and placing it in the warm oven.

Spread out on the counters of the kitchen were the spoils from Margie's trip to Winn-Dixie earlier in the day. She set the ham on the butcher block work island in the middle of the kitchen, along with several jars of orange marmalade and Dijon mustard.

Before continuing, she took a couple of deep breaths and poured a glass of Relax Riesling.

The thirteen-inch television in the corner of the kitchen sat noiselessly projecting waves of blue and white light, the word MUTE appearing in the right hand corner. The cajun chef himself, Justin Wilson, was coming on. Margie clutched the remote control and turned up the sound.

She loved Justin. The man had style. Today he was preparing an exotic dish and was talking about it while holding an onion. Justin called it an "ahhhn-yohn." He explained how the onion had to be prepared and placed in the pot, and that the cook must use the entire onion: "Dat whole *damn* ahhn-yohn!" Justin exhorted.

Margie giggled, and with her best coon-ass inflection, stated to the television, "You tell 'em, Justin. Make'em use that whole *damn* ahhn-yohn!"

Margie took another sip of wine. This was going to be a good day. Sometimes–*especially* when she had some good wine–Margie would let herself drift away as she cooked, concentrating on the good feelings that she associated with being in the kitchen. When she was in one of these moods she often lost track of the time.

The ham was a beaut. She wiped it down thoroughly with damp paper towels, selected a fillet knife, and began scoring it, preferring a diagonal pattern. Next, she transferred the ham to a roasting pan, took the cast iron pot out of the warm oven, and slid the ham inside. Using a small pottery bowl, Margie spooned in equal amounts of the orange marmalade, honey, and mustard, stirring them into a uniform amber glaze. She then placed a glaze brush into the bowl and set it on the stove.

Laughing at Justin and sipping her wine–she was going on her second glass–Margie sorted through the rest of the grocery bags. She put the sweet potatoes into a wire basket in the pantry, the stone ground corn meal into the freezer, and the bottles of cooking sherry onto the counter because she just liked the way they looked there.

According to Justin, one should not cook with anything that one would not like to drink. Margie followed his advice and always ended up driving to her favorite liquor store on Ocean Drive. The building featured a mural depicting an ocean scene and palm trees on one entire wall, complete with a sandwich board sign proclaiming "WE SELL HOLIDAY CHEER!"

Holiday cheer, indeed.

That made Margie smile almost every time she saw it. She always ended up perusing the medium-priced wines until she found some bottles that she thought would look nice lined up on her kitchen counters.

A little tipsy, Margie thought that life was a feast! Her kitchen was her queendom! It was the one area in her life and her home where she could impose order her way. She assessed the liquor bottles for proper appearance and placed the rest of the bottles and cans in their appointed places on the pantry shelves. She then sat down with a notebook and pen and proceeded to create her culinary schedule for the evening.

On the menu were sweet potato pies. Those would be placed on the bottom shelves while the ham baked. Four, perhaps five of them. When Lance got home he would dive into one for sure (after violating her orders and cutting off a piece of the ham). After dinner, she would have Lance carve the most succulent portions of the ham so that they could eat it, and then save the rest for the holiday festivities.

Lance would also be in charge of trimming the bones and cracking them with a hammer. The ham bones, along with some of the ham scraps, would be needed to make stock for the red beans and rice. Such a dish was required at all family functions, along with skillet cornbread and sweet potato pie.

Margie took another sip of wine, draining the glass. Everything was put away and ready to go. She looked around the house. It was clean. She had just about run out of busy work to do while waiting for Lance to come back with the water hoses. Actually, she just wanted him back home.

The house was lonely and quiet...and she was having *thoughts*.

She thought about him. Lance was still as funny and charming as he was when they first married. Things were going well. She gave him enough rope so that he could enjoy himself with the boys, but the truth was she enjoyed him now more than ever. Their marriage had been free of major turbulence for a long time and she liked it that way.

But it also made her feel a little uneasy.

She had been bracing for some sort of marital calamity for the last few months, but it never came. It had just gotten better and better, and she wanted it to continue. That is why she set down her wine glass and frowned as she looked out the kitchen window and into the empty driveway.

Lance had been so good and sweet to her the last few months. She wondered if he was due to sow some wild oats. He had been out with his friends last night, though. The thing was, Lance could not really hold his liquor that well. She knew. His complaints about hangovers and sickness were not idle. If he complained about being sick or having a hangover, it was the real deal. It really did take Lance a few days to recover from a serious bender like last night. Margie thought that he should have been home by now, whining to go to bed.

She would lead him into the bedroom if he would only come home.

Margie picked up the remote, clicked off Justin, picked up her cell and dialed Lance. It rang about five times before Lance's voice came on the line, "Hey, this is Lance, leave a message."

Crap.

Voice mail. Margie waited for the tone and then spoke into her phone, "Hey Bob Villa, get those hoses and get your butt home. I'm kind of interested in your hose right now. Love ya, bye." She hit the END button.

Beneath the wine-mood, she was a little bit irked because she had told him a thousand times to make sure that his phone was on when he had it with him because, really, what good did it do to have a phone if she could not get hold of him? He usually *did* have it on. In fact, she could not ever remember him having the phone off because he *knew* how much it annoyed her.

Then she recalled that he said that he may stop by the office. Maybe he was having some sort of meeting and had turned it off.

Margie looked at her empty wine glass and then at the almost-empty wine bottle.

Might was well finish it off.

She poured the rest of the wine into her glass and then placed the dead soldier in the glass recycle bin. She took a sip and sat in the kitchen for a few minutes, taking in the aromas and trying to remember if there was something she was forgetting to do. She could think of nothing. Justin was still on when she pressed the POWER button on the TV remote. She figured she had enough time to make some potato salad before Lance made it home.

If he wanted to get lucky with her, he would have to hurry.

PART II
BLACK PAVILION

Pleaseth your mightiness to understand,
His resolution far exceedeth all.
The first day when he pitcheth down his tents,
White is their hue, and on his silver crest
A snowy feather spangled-white he bears,
To signify the mildness of his mind,
That, satiate with spoil, refuseth blood:
But, when Aurora mounts the second time,
As red as scarlet is his furniture;
Then must his kindled wrath be quench'd with blood,
Not sparing any that can manage arms:
But, if these threats move not submission,
Black are his colours, black pavilion;
His spear, his shield, his horse, his armour, plumes,
And jetty feathers, menace death and hell;
Without respect of sex, degree, or age,
He razeth all his foes with fire and sword.

–Christopher Marlowe, *Tamburlaine the Great* (1587),
Part 1, Act IV, Scene I

CHAPTER TWENTY-THREE

Walter looked at his reflection in the men's room mirror.

Under his right eye, a long flap of skin hung vertically down his face, resting heavily on his cheek. He could sense the weight of it, but he did not feel pain in the usual way. Walter's perception changed from moment to moment in wave-like bursts, as if his comprehension of reality was regulated by tidal forces.

He perceived the pain from the wound on his face, and to a lesser extent his ankle, as bright colors that changed with each beat of his heart. The colors were irritating and distracting, a warning of some sort that remained unclear; beyond them, as he looked at his reflection in the mirror, the change in facial symmetry as a result of the wound caused Walter to feel that perhaps he was seeing his own face for the first time.

The colors in his head were a mystery. He was unsure how to react to them, but he reacted to the wound itself by pressing the loose flap of skin back in place on his cheek. On his way to the men's room he had passed a green-colored industrial first aid kit–which he recognized by the universal red cross on the lid–mounted on the wall by a circular saw at the end of the last lumber aisle. He had grabbed the kit and took it with him into the men's room. As Walter pressed the skin-flap in place, he secured it with several butterfly band-aids from the kit.

The visual effect was dramatic.

Although the colors still pulsed in his head, they had dimmed to a point where he could see clearly and, as he looked into the mirror, it appeared as if there was no wound there at all. He blinked a few times, taking in the odd sensation he felt on the right side of his face. Walter's right eye was swelling, but his vision was clear.

Despite the visual comfort of the first aid treatment, Walter still felt the sickness *inside* his head, gnawing away at his brain. At his *mind*.

When he had been at Spring Hill, he had perceived it as *pressure* inside his head; pressure that he had not been able to endure any longer.

The guard at Spring Hill–

Bones? Jones?

–had meant to take him back to Jackson this morning. Jackson. Where it had all begun. His mother had tried to shield him from it by moving him to the Gulf, but it had eventually caught up with her.

Walter had not wanted to hurt her, but in the end he had had no choice. When the guard had come for him this morning, Walter had sensed that relocation was an obvious trap, although the guard was not part of it.

He was just a tool.

Walter had considered killing him anyway and escaping, but after Walter had handed him the money and asked for a cigarette, the guard had unshackled Walter and allowed him to walk away.

Walter considered this divine providence.

He was clearly meant to face his enemy right here and now; and he was ready to make his stand. He was in a fight. A *good* fight.

One that would have *resolution*.

The architecture of Walter's delusions allowed him to perceive that, because the Phoebe-thing had survived the first encounter (the one in this very building but a few years ago), it had proven itself strong and resourceful. It had in fact retaliated against Walter by seizing his mind, trying to penetrate into his thoughts and control his actions. It was formidable. If he was able to destroy this enemy, its grip would be broken and the haze in his mind would clear.

It would *have* to clear.

Walter marched in place like a toy soldier, testing his ankle. He was injured. The colors flared when he put his weight on it, but it held his weight. He looked inside the kit for something to brace the ankle but there was nothing.

As he planted his weight on the leg with the injured ankle he was treated to a visual spray of vivid colors. He focused on the red, trying to use it to conceptualize his plan of attack. He knew that he must attack but it was difficult to conceive how it must be done. In the past, he had been able to internalize multiple abstract ideas and thoughts at once with little effort. Now he wondered if his mind had gone too soft at the Hill; if he had retreated within it too often, or too deep, when he had nothing to occupy it.

He stared into the mirror, noticing yet another wound to his head–the one where the Phoebe-thing had hit him with the metal nut.

He saw that a single red line of brightly hued blood–*his* blood–was trailing down his right cheek from under the dressing he had just applied. It appeared to Walter as a single, long, red teardrop, as if representing all the tears that he had ever cried out of hate and misery and, now most of all, *vengeance.* He moved his hands toward the first aid kit to retrieve another dressing, but then stopped.

then must his kindled wrath be quench'd with blood

Who had said that? He had known at one time but could no longer remember. He tried to sink down into the grids to retrieve it, but there was only a flicker. The name could not be found, but he realized that it was from the story of the tents; and how they went from white, to red, and then finally to black.

Black pavilion.

As with many things Walter had seen over the last several days, he looked again at the bloody tear running down his face and took it as a sign. It told him that he was in a blood game.

And that it was time to play.

CHAPTER TWENTY-FOUR

Lance surveyed the back wall of the store from his position atop the lumber stacks. He had considered just staying up there until the damn store opened again, but he feared that it would be Monday before that happened. That would be *four* nights up there by himself all alone.

Well, not *entirely* alone.

After some time went by and Lance was able to actually *think,* he concluded that, however this situation was going to be resolved, it was going to happen prior to the expiration of four nights. He could not just sit up there and bide his time. He had to take action. Offense, as they say, is the best defense.

But what kind of offense?

Because of the way in which the front of the store was sealed off, Lance did not hold out any hope that he would be able to simply walk out the back door. He told himself that he had to assume at this point that the back doors were locked and sealed also (but at some point he might have to take his chances back there).

That left the phones.

His own phone was shot. Useless. He was tempted to make a run for the front anyway because there was bound to be a working landline up there at one of the stations. He hesitated because he had not noticed any hiding places up there. But now he wasn't even sure about that. When he had walked in the store looking to purchase garden hoses, he hadn't really paid attention to the layout up front for purposes of hiding from maul-wielding maniacs while help arrived. It had not crossed his mind at the time.

In fact, Lance had become painfully aware of just how little he had paid attention to the details of the store, even though he had been inside of it hundreds of times over the years.

He was certain that if he made a break for the front, the nutcase in here with him would notice. Lance doubted that he could make it up there quietly; and of course he could be seen easily once he started to climb down. Lance figured that he could run to the front and *make the call* with no problem. The problem was what would happen then? If there was no shelter up front, could he survive another close-quarters encounter with the man while waiting for help to arrive?

He didn't think so.

He'd be dead by the time the cops got here, the whole thing recorded live on a 911 audiotape–or better yet a store video surveillance tape–for some ghoul to post on the internet for all of the other ghouls to enjoy.

He was stuck like chuck. Hiding out atop the lumber stacks for the duration of this ordeal was not an option, but at least he felt *safe* there for the time being. That safe feeling was an extremely powerful motivator to stay put.

If the front was out of the question, and staying put indefinitely was not an option, that left the back. Lance kept glancing at the door about halfway down the back wall of the store, and the long rectangular window just after it. Further down was a hallway that led to the back of the store. The entrance to the men's room was inside that hallway.

Lance surmised that the room behind the door and long window must be the manager's office; and that inside would have to be a telephone.

If he could get in there quietly and without being seen, he could simply call the police and wait in the office for the cavalry to arrive. Lance liked this idea. The main problem was that the door might be locked. If it was, then he was probably in for a long night and an extremely nasty confrontation.

Despite the man's actions, Lance did not want to have to kill him. Did not want to be *pushed* to that extreme.

If the office door was locked…well then, he could think of no other options. He would have to find a weapon if he could, go to the back of the store, and hope to find an exit. Finding weapons in this place was easy. They were everywhere he looked. Lance's concern was that he did not know himself as well as he had thought. He was unsure how far he could take it. If it came to a mano-a-mano fight to the end, he was not sure if he had the kind of instinct needed to finish it. He was also sure that the other man *did*.

But if the door *was* open, then there was a good chance of getting home tonight and sleeping in his own bed. Next to Margie.

He felt a warm droplet hit his hand.

He had not even realized that just thinking about being home with Margie had brought him to tears again. He had arrived here ill from drunkenness and food poisoning, had been assaulted and injured by a lunatic, and now simply wanted to go home. He felt deep fatigue beginning to take hold of him, a loss of the edge that had come with the adrenaline rushes. Lance had a feeling that he would come down hard very soon. His tired old out-of-shape body could take only so much.

That is why, in the end, Lance decided to call the authorities from the manager's office. He wanted out of this situation; wanted to go home and feel his wife in his arms again. Wanted to feel *safe* again.

The longer this situation dragged on, the worse his chances. If there was to be a final and decisive confrontation, it would be much better for him if it happened sooner rather than later.

Sooner, he had a shot. Maybe not a *good* shot, but a shot.

Later…well, he was forced to come to grips with that. If he had to fight the man later, chances were good that he would end up like a fighting rooster on the losing end of a money match. *Dead cock in the pit.*

He had a memory of going to the cockfights with his grandfather, Papa Tom. Lance must have been about twelve. His parents would not have allowed it, but he had been staying with Papa Tom for about a week for some reason that he could not recall. One day, Papa Tom asked Lance if he had ever been the cockfights. Lance had said, "No, sir."

"Well, let's go."

They had loaded up in Papa Tom's old Dodge and driven out to a farm in the middle of nowhere.

Lance remembered the noises of the place. The shouting. The excitement. The *anticipation.* Papa Tom never did have any fighting cocks of his own, but he did have a wad of cash that he kept in the front pocket of his bib overalls. The wad came out when it had been time to make the bets. Lance had not understood how all that had worked. He had been too transfixed on how the fowl were fitted with metal spurs and made to confront one another in the hands of their handlers before being let go to fight for real.

Even after watching the pre-fight spectacle, it had never occurred to Lance that the fights were to the death. It had only dawned on him when he had seen one of the gamecocks floundering in the pit amid the screaming, cheering spectators–he and his granddaddy included–and then the blood from the animal followed by a series of twitches that tapered off to stillness.

"DEAD COCK IN THE PIT!"–

–had been the cry of the house man who had declared the match over. This was the official signal for the money to trade hands and for the next match to begin. Lance had not quite known what to think about what he had seen, but Papa Tom and the rest of the spectators seemed to think that the fight had been a good one.

On that score, Lance had been in agreement, but he never wanted to go back to the cockfights (nor did Papa Tom ever ask again). Lance never wanted to see that dead cock in the pit again. That lonely dead bird too weak to survive.

Sitting cross-legged on the lumber stacks, Lance thought back to that time long ago, and to the image of the exhausted and bloody rooster laying motionless in the circular arena.

"Dead cock in the pit," Lance whispered.

Lance tilted his head and listened for a few minutes to the sounds of the building, trying to listen for any sign of the man. Hearing none, Lance stood up and got his bearings in the semi-darkness.

He began to climb down.

CHAPTER TWENTY-FIVE

Bruce the Deuce (sometimes also known as Bruce the Douche) sat in his cubicle at Petra Energy, pondering what Lance had just said about checking for the data sheets in Vernie's office. It was dark on his side of the cubicle except for the illumination from his computer monitor. Bruce preferred to work in the dark if he could because he was prone to headaches and it eased the tension.

He was alone at the office as usual.

Bruce was working on a couple of different projects, busy make-work stuff mostly, although if he could locate the data sheets that Lance Davis was supposed to have provided he might be able to get some *real* work done.

Work that might get him noticed.

Work that would make Mr. Jarrett *very* happy. Bruce hated having to rely on other people in order to get things done, and the worst was that fuckhead Lance. Lance was a loafer. Dead weight, along with pretty much everyone else who worked at the office in Bruce's opinion. They were a bunch of clockwatchers just waiting to flee out the door at five o'clock so they could go directly home to their ugly spouses, their reclining easy chairs, and watch whatever idiocy that was on the Boob Tube.

Bruce wondered how corporate America survived at all. Take his office, for example. It was the Peter Principle in action. The only two workers in the office with actual offices rather than cubicles were Lance and Vernie (other than the Big Boss himself and Mr. Jarrett, of course), and they were the two most worthless employees on the payroll.

Take the data sheet issue, for example. Lance had no clue how important those were, and just how good a product could be created with them, and in turn given to Mr. Jarrett (with a cc to the Big Boss, too; Mr. Jarrett was a good guy, but no sense in risking that one would not get proper credit for one's work, and not even Mr. Jarrett was above passing off the work of others as his own if the situation arose). Lame-ass Lance (as Bruce liked to call him) not only could not find them, he had–and this is the *funny* part, the real *howler*–suggested that they might be in Vernie's office.

Bruce wondered again how this place even functioned without the extra work that he put in. Here he was, the only one at the office, and Idiot Number One's only suggestion to him on how to find important documents was to look in the office of Idiot Number Two. Both of their offices were locked (of course), thus leaving the only actual worker at the office with no way to obtain what he needed to do the work.

Business as usual.

It did not even sound like Lance was at home. He was probably out with Frank and Carl doing any stupid thing possible to get arrested and fired. Bruce was not surprised. Lance was the only one in the office who actually had a reason to go home. That sexy wife of his was probably sick of his shit, too. Bruce had no idea how a schmuck like Lance had landed that one. It made perfect sense that he would be out with the two degenerates in the office rather than at home nailing his old lady.

Bruce put his hands behind his head and leaned back in his chair.

The basic question was whether it would be best to make Lance look as incompetent as he was, or whether he should make himself look good. There were pros and cons to both.

If he found the data sheets in Vernie's office and completed everything by Monday then there would be no doubt that Mr. Jarrett and the Big Boss would be impressed. Bruce could probably get the cleaning people or the security up there to open Vernie's office.

But letting Lance twist in the wind had appeal as well. Bruce suspected that Mr. Jarrett did not especially like Lance, or that creep Carl Sanders who was always loitering around in Lance's office. Bruce's stock would definitely go up if he applied a little elbow grease this weekend and got some work done, but what did he want more? His stock to rise at the moment, or Lance's stock to go down?

Tumbling those above him was almost as good as rising himself.

It sure would be sweet to make Lance look like an idiot.

And perhaps, just maybe, get him fired.

Mr. Jarrett was already concerned that Lance could not find the data sheets. The dumb shit did not even seem to care that much this morning when he had been asked about it, and Bruce did not think that Lance appreciated fully the severity of the situation. Bruce knew that Mr. Jarrett was catching heat from above, and that Lance did not seem to have a clue. If Bruce were to explain to Mr. Jarrett on Monday morning that he *could have* gotten everything done over the weekend, *the Fourth of July holiday weekend no less*, but had been unable to do so because Lance had not called him back with the location of the data sheets, well then ol' Lance would have his tit tightly in the wringer.

Yes, sir.

Bruce smiled at the idea of Lance tap dancing in Mr. Jarrett's office, trying to explain that the data sheets were in Vernie's office and that it really was not his fault. The beauty of it was that even if the data really were in Vernie's office, it would, of course, be too late. Lance had fucked up and wasted a lot of time because of his irresponsible handling of the data sheets. Bruce could then commiserate with Mr. Jarrett about the lack of dedication of some employees in the office.

Yes, there were certainly some options available here.

On the whole, Bruce leaned toward making himself look good. The Lord helps those who help themselves. Plus, Bruce did not have anything better to do this weekend. It was really no skin off his nose to get everything in order by Monday. It would, in fact, be pretty easy.

Bruce's long-term goals included, of course, taking over Mr. Jarrett's job. Mr. Jarrett was competent, but c'mon, what kind of middle manager left the office for four straight days? Not a dedicated one, that's for sure.

Bruce suspected that Lance was dumb enough to get himself fired without any help. If Bruce did not fan the flames this time, there would be other incidents that would come up with that guy. It was only a matter of time. Bruce clicked on the web browser of his computer and checked his e-mail.

Nothing.

He thought about what to do. The first thing would be to check Vernie's office and verify that the data sheets were actually there. That would take care of a lot of his options right there. If the data sheets were there, then he would have to make a decision, although he had *almost* resolved to just finish the work.

But if the stuff wasn't in Vernie's office, then there was not much that he could do. It would be tap dance city for ol' Lance on Monday morning.

Bruce got out of his chair and walked down the deserted hall toward Vernie's office. He turned the door knob. Locked like he thought it would be. It was maddening that he did not have a key. He was the only one who stayed late and worked weekends for Christ's sake. He should have access to the other offices in case he needed something. He would discuss the situation with Mr. Jarrett on Monday.

Bruce walked back to his cubicle and brought up the company directory. He looked up Lance's cell phone number for the second time in the last half hour and punched the numbers on the key pad. After several rings he was transferred to Lance's voice mail where he left a message for Lance to call him back at the office. But Bruce was sure that the dumb shit had turned his phone off after Bruce had called him.

Well, that's what the lazy prick gets.

"Don't say that I didn't try to help you, pal." Bruce said aloud in the empty office as he set the phone back into the cradle.

CHAPTER TWENTY-SIX

Margie opened her eyes. She was disoriented and had to focus on where she was. Her eyelids felt very heavy and she was still for a few minutes until the cobwebs cleared. She was on the couch in the living room. After she had finished things in the kitchen (and the bottle of wine, don't forget that), she had taken a little nap. She sat up, listening to the sounds of the house. Listening for sounds of Lance.

Nothing.

The house was quiet except for the humming of the central air and the low chatter of the kitchen televison which was still turned on, but had been turned way down. Margie blinked the sleep out of her eyes and stretched out as she got off the couch and went to the front room to look out the window. Lance's car was not in the driveway. She glanced at the clock on the mantel. She had only been sleeping for forty minutes, but it seemed much longer than that. She stretched out again and tried to think if he had said he would be late. She did not recall anything like that.

Where the hell was Lance?

She was starting to get annoyed. He had better get his butt back home soon before he turned her case of amused annoyance into a case of full blown pissed off irritation. It just wasn't like him to do this to her. She walked from the living room into the kitchen and looked out the window to see if he was on his way.

No sign of him.

She went into the kitchen and filled up a water glass from the refrigerator with lots of ice and cold water. She drank it deeply and then filled it back up and drank some more. Her wine-buzz was gone, and so was the friskiness that had come along for the ride. Pity Lance had not made it home.

Margie grabbed her cell and tried to call Lance. Just the voice mail again. This time, she did not leave a message. Instead, she disconnected from his cell number and dialed the back-line office number in order to avoid the answering service. On the fifth ring, a voice answered.

"Hello? Lance?" The voice on the other end of the line was hesitant. Margie was confused for a second.

This person thinks that Lance is calling them?

She replied, "No, this is actually Marge Davis, Lance's wife."

"Oh, hi Marge! This is Bruce. Bruce Rigsby. I had just called Lance's cell phone a little while ago and I thought that maybe this was him calling me back."

Bruce Rigsby?

Margie did not recall him specifically, but had a vague idea that Lance did not like him. Margie gave a polite laugh into the phone, "Well, isn't that odd, I just tried to call him, too, and thought that maybe he was up at the office. He said he may stop by."

"No, he hasn't been back since he left this morning," Bruce said. "But, hey, if you talk to him this evening, tell him to give me a call up here would you please?"

"Okay, I will. You have a good Fourth, Bruce."

"Thanks, and same to you Marge, bye-bye." Bruce hung up the phone.

Margie stood in the kitchen looking perplexed. How odd. Lance had turned off his cell, and not only was he not at the office, he had apparently not even gone to the office like he said he might. If Lance had only gone to the *Emporium*, he should have been home by now.

Long before now in fact.

Margie's radar was beginning to pick up some very bad signals that there could be some tomfoolery afoot.

At the office, Bruce chuckled as he hung up the phone. He couldn't help it. He knew he had just blown Lance's cover with his old lady.

Sure, Margie, I'm gonna be up at the office for a while, wink, wink.

That's what the jackass deserved for not calling him back or finding the files. He was probably out with Creepy Carl, slacking as usual.

Bruce hoped that he had a good story made up for Margie by the time he staggered back home.

CHAPTER TWENTY-SEVEN

Lance moved slowly down the lumber stacks, descending in a tensed-crouch while looking down each side of the aisle in rapid, neck-swiveling succession. As his right foot landed softly on the concrete floor, Lance planted his left beside it and let go of the steel beam. The climb down had taken a long time and Lance was sweating and tired from the exertion. He stood in the center of the aisle feeling exposed.

Very exposed.

It was bad *feng shui*. From his position in the middle of the aisle, Lance could not monitor both ends at the same time. He constantly looked down one end and then the other, making sure that the man had not spotted him.

As Lance stood once again on firm ground, his heart thudded in his chest as he continued to look down one end of the aisle and then back to the opposite end. He had felt so vulnerable on the climb down; and the feeling had not left him once he was on the ground.

After Lance glanced up and down the aisle about five times to make sure the man was not around, he relaxed a little bit. No sign of him. Lance stood still for a moment, listening.

Nothing.

As he stood stock-still in the aisle, the injured finger on his left hand started to bleed again as the result of his efforts during the climb down. He could feel his heartbeat rhythm in his fingertip as it throbbed. He took a few small, careful steps down the aisle, walking toward the back of the store so that he could peek around the corner and surveil the area by the office door. Or at least what he *hoped* was the office door.

It looked clear.

Lance could neither see nor hear the man and had no idea where he could be. His best guess was that maybe the man was in the men's room tending to the nasty wound on his face. That's where Lance would have gone if it had been him.

Yeah. If I was a crazy homicidal maniac and some bastard had just peeled half my face I'd probably go clean it up in the john.

Lance paused. The men's room was very close to the door to the office, about thirty feet further down from where Lance was standing. His plan was to walk to the office door, open it, go inside and use the phone.

But what if the man *was* in the john?

If he was, and decided to come out right now, he would catch Lance unarmed and defenseless. There would be no way that Lance could scurry back up to the top of the lumber stacks again. The man would be able to easily grab him from behind and pull him down.

Lance was once again paralyzed with indecision.

This must be what rabbits feel like in the headlights of an oncoming car.

Which way to go? To the office that might not be an office to use a phone that might not be there? Or back to the stacks to wait it out? Part of his mind chided him for climbing down.

Are you nuts? Why go looking for trouble? Just hide from the crazy son of a bitch. Stay on top of the stacks and just chill.

But his instincts for self-preservation ignored that voice. He had been over all that. He could not hide in this place for four straight days and nights.

But someone would notice your car and help would arrive much earlier than that.

Lance cut it off. He had already decided. He had to act. Lance took a deep breath, held it, and released it slowly and quietly as he took a step out in the open toward the office door.

Fully exposed now, Lance took big, careful steps, looking in all directions as he went. So far, so good. Halfway there he heard a sound and stopped in his tracks, heart thumping, his breath coming in shallow waves. Something was moving straight down the aisle and, from the sound of it, it was high. His mind reeled. It felt like he had stepped into a trap.

Could he also have climbed up on top of an aisle without me knowing about it? Is he looking down on me right now?

Although in reality his breathing was not loud at all, it seemed to Lance that he was breathing very loudly. This began a vicious self-compounding cycle where his loud breathing fed his panic, and his panic in turn affected his breathing. It became more pronounced the more he tried to control it. Lance was in real danger of hyperventilating and passing out.

He looked in the direction of the sound and saw that it was just a bird that had made a nest in one of the overhead beams. Lance could not believe it.

This place is large enough for a bird to nest?

It seemed unbelievable. Lance was able to calm down a bit. He knew that he was doomed if he went into an outright panic and fainted. Easy does it. As he stepped closer to the door of the office–he was now not more than five feet away–he heard another sound. But this one he recognized immediately.

It was the sound of running water, and it was coming from the men's room.

The man had to be in there. Who else could have turned on the faucet? Lance was sure that when he left there after his diarrhetic debacle he had turned off the faucet.

The man was in there!

The specter of the man opening the door and rushing out to kill him flashed instantly in his mind. But it was followed immediately by an exhilarating thought.

He doesn't know that I'm here.

Lance had the element of surprise. If he was in there now–and Lance was convinced that he was–then he did not know that Lance *knew* that he was in there. The primitive module of Lance's brain quickly sprang into life.

Ambush.

Attack that son of a bitch and take him out. *Find a weapon, a big nasty one, say, a maul, for instance, and just stand outside the door and cleave him in half when he comes out. You want to survive, don't you? Well, pardner, this is survival central talking to you here and a man has to do what a man has to do.*

Lance considered this as he stood there, again torn by the possibilities. He would have to go find a suitable weapon first, and then double back before the man came out. The man himself may still have a weapon. There was no guarantee that this would work.

But the main reason that Lance rejected that inner voice was because, well, that voice emanated from a place and time where men killed, hunted and gathered, and dragged their mates by the hair, kicking and screaming into the caves. With Lance, there had simply been too many layers of civilization and socialization instilled in his personality for him to stand outside the john and commit the brutal and premeditated murder of another human being. He was not a killer. Lance knew that, in the end, he would balk, and that would spell disaster because he was quite sure that the other man would not. Lance could not murder this man.

He was mere feet away from the office door.

Lance walked toward the door and put his hand on the knob.

Please, God, let it be unlocked.

He did not want to think about what he might have to do if the door was locked. The knob turned easily in his hand. Lance pushed the door open as quietly as he could and stepped inside the office of Assistant Manager Randy Philpot. Lance turned to close the door behind him but held it open a crack, put his ear to the open space, and listened for any movement outside.

No sound at all.

The running water had stopped.

Lance closed the door, being careful to turn the knob and then close it flush in order to prevent the sound of the door latch as it sprung forward into the jamb. Still squatting, Lance looked around the office.

The room had no character or style. There was only a desk (the pre-assembled kind), a cheap chair, and an ancient filing cabinet set against the back wall. The filing cabinet was a big one; it looked to be about as tall as Lance. A calendar hung from a nail on the wall and that was the only decor in the whole room.

As his eyes adjusted to his dimly lit surroundings, Lance also saw another door on the far side of the office, directly behind the desk. That had possibilities. Lance guessed that it led directly into the back of the store. It *must* lead to the back so that the manager could to go check on stuff back there. He supposed it could be a closet, but this place did not look like it had any such amenities. Everything was functional.

Although Lance was sure that the sun must be setting now, there was still just enough light in the store to get around. Lance had a sinking feeling as he looked across the room at the phone sitting on the desk. There *was* a phone. That was the good news. But what caused the sinking feeling was the fact that the phone was positioned on the far edge of the desk.

Lance realized that, in the normal course of business, the person in this office would position himself in clear view of anyone outside the window. Whoever it was that normally occupied this office would not mind such exposure; in fact, they probably would like it because it would allow them to see what was going on in the store.

Lance crouched down behind the door and wondered how to proceed. He was now eye level with the door knob. It had one of those push button mechanisms located in the middle of the knob that allowed the door to be locked. Lance did not think that it would keep the man out if he was seen (and of course the window could be easily broken), but it may buy him some time. So, he pushed the button slowly and locked the door.

He turned and looked at the desk, and then at the window. The window began about four feet off the ground. Lance saw that he could crawl directly under the window and over to the phone without being seen. The lights were off in the office, thank God, and Lance did not think that if the man peered in the window that he could be seen if he were hiding directly under it.

But there appeared to be no way around the problem of actually using the phone. He would have to expose himself to discovery if he tried it. And he had no idea when the man was going to leave the men's room.

He may have already.

Lance began to crawl on his hands and knees against the wall beneath the window and toward the end of the desk where the phone, and hopefully help, waited.

CHAPTER TWENTY-EIGHT

Walter turned the water faucet off and dried his hands with a paper towel from the dispenser. He was ready now. There was no hurry. It was still out there. Gathering strength and waiting.

So am I.

The preliminaries were over. It was probably still up on top of the wood pile where he had left it. Maybe the showdown would take place up there. He was going to find out.

Was going to find out *toot fucking sweet*.

He opened the door to the men's room slowly. Just in

case. No one was waiting. He walked out. There was no movement and no sound on the main aisle along the back wall.

He had been foolish to climb up the lumber stacks. He now understood the positional advantage of defending from the top while he tried to ascend. He had learned a good lesson. Even at the time he had attacked, he had known better. He had just been overcome and not thinking clearly.

In fact, he had been in a little bit of a frenzy.

Plus, at the time, he was so close. It had barely escaped his grasp. But he had learned his lesson. The colors that danced with each throb in his face were reminders.

Walter tried to retreat into the grids in his mind. They usually helped him in these situations, but as he tried to climb them the bottom gave way to darkness and Walter tumbled down, not knowing if he would ever be able to stop.

He was out on his feet for a few seconds, during which his eyes fixed and he swayed back and forth like a drunkard trying to recall something important. When Walter came back, he looked around, momentarily confused as to where he was and why he was there. He remembered walking out of the men's room just then. He was dimly aware that Frankie had hurt him somewhere. Somewhere on his face. Probably got help from his lap dog Grady and that coward Ronnie. Walter had no problem devising his revenge now. It came swiftly. Frankie had finally retaliated and now the game was really on.

If Frankie wanted to climb on top of the lumber stacks to try to avoid him, well two could play at that game. Walter could climb, too. Only when Walter went up, he would have some surprises ready.

Oh yes, some very *harsh* surprises in store for Frankie, and Grady, too. Frankie had actually tried to *kill* him with a fucking two-by-four. Did he think that Walter was just going to go away? If so, Frankie had another thing coming. Missing teeth and a split lip were going to be the least of his problems.

Walter surveyed the store in his mind for a moment longer and made up his mind to proceed to the large display case near the front that contained the collection of knives. He had just the perfect one in mind. His original choice had been a long garden claw near the mauls. Walter had just liked the looks of it. It was long like a hoe, but instead of only a straight metal blade, it had three wicked looking *claws* on the end.

However, since the incident with the board crashing into his face–*peeling his face*–Walter had changed his mind from the garden claw toward a large, serrated filet knife that he had seen in the knife case. It would be more–

intimate

He needed to *see* Frankie up close this time.

Walter took a step toward the front of the store, one hand holding the gauze on his cheek and the other gripping the small hatchet that he had taken into the men's room with him. There was still plenty of time to...

Click!

Walter stopped in mid-step and turned his head toward the sound. It was close. *Real* close. He looked in the direction from where the sound had emanated and zeroed in on a door along the back wall.

At the Hill, all doors were locked all the time (except, say, when a small favor was granted by a guard to an appreciative patient). Almost all the doors had heavy deadbolts, but they were also fitted with the large round metal knobs with the push-in type locking mechanism. During his four years at the Hill, Walter had heard that sound a million times. The little *click* when the guard pushed the button in to lock the door.

He would know that sound anywhere.

And he had just heard it from the door just down from the men's room, about twenty feet from where he stood.

CHAPTER TWENTY-NINE

Lance finally worked up the nerve to lean over, grab the phone off the desk, and pull it towards him as he crouched in the corner of the office. As he did so, a small object slid with the phone and landed on the floor. He scooted the object towards his body with his foot, picked it up, and saw that it was a book of matches. Without really thinking about it, he put it in his pocket. He turned his attention to the beautiful, magnificent phone.

He took a few deep breaths. He was excited again, absolutely *elated* this time. This had to be done right. He may not get another chance. He picked up the handset and put it to his ear.

Nothing.

Not to worry. Lance used a similar business model phone system at his office. There were about ten different buttons and he had to push one of them to get an outside line, that was all. It was difficult to see in the dimly lit little office. He looked carefully at the descriptions next to the buttons. One of them was marked PA--ANNOUNCE.

Oh shit, how funny would *that* be? He imagined pushing that button and having his voice electronically amplified through the store-wide PA system.

Attention Emporium shoppers and homicidal maniacs! This holiday weekend only The Builder's Emporium has marked select merchandise wayyyyy down for the Fourth of July! We have nails marked down to a dollar a box! Mauls for five dollars! Stock up on these items and more for your senseless killing needs!

Lance skipped the PA button and pressed the button marked LINE 1.

A small green light came on and Lance placed his thumb over it in order to hide the light from view. The wondrous, soothing, hopeful sound of a dial tone filled his right ear. A wall of emotion hit Lance–a relief so intense that it brought him close to tears. He had been holding his breath the entire time he was pushing buttons and slowly let it out, so grateful that he would be able to summon someone to help him escape from this nightmare.

He pressed 9-1-1 and waited.

And waited. It seemed like an eternity. Lance nearly went into shock as his end of the phone filled with the loud and incessant universal tone of a *busy* signal.

He started to panic.

They can't be busy! They absolutely can't be! 9-1-1 can't be inaccessible to people who have emergencies! They can't! Christ, I pay my taxes! I have called the proverbial fucking suicide hotline and gotten a busy signal!

He depressed the phone's hang up switch with his finger, disconnected from the line, and tried to collect himself.

Think.

What had he done? He had pressed the button marked LINE 1 and had gotten an outside line to make a phone call.

Outside line.

Okay, that's it. Probably just had to dial nine first to get an outside line.

Okay, buddy, calm down, just dial nine for an outside line and the cavalry will be on its...

Someone was trying to get into the office.

Lance's breath caught in his throat and thick tentacles of black panic squeezed his chest. Someone was standing outside the office door trying to turn the knob. Lance had the phone's handset cocked between his ear and his shoulder, his forefinger still depressed on the hang up switch, and his thumb covering the glowing green light emanating from the face of the phone.

There were no sounds coming from the phone and Lance made none except the ragged breath that was now going in and out of his lungs in little wheezes. He saw the knob turn slowly one way and then back the other way. It did not turn very much. Lance was frozen with terror. He was caught and he was absolutely defenseless.

But I locked it!

That's right. He did recall that he had locked it.

Maybe he'll go away. If I sit tight and do not panic, he'll just move on.

For a moment it seemed possible. Lance did not move a muscle. *Could* not move a muscle. He was still paralyzed with fear and was now starting to hyperventilate.

The knob stopped moving.

Lance heard the man shuffle his feet outside the door and over toward the window.

Toward Lance.

Lance almost screamed when the man walked to the window and cast a long shadow across the inside of the office. The man was standing outside the window and looking in with his hands cupped on both sides of his head. If the window and the wall partition were removed instantly by magic, Lance would be at the man's feet. Lance looked up and noticed that the man had somehow managed to find a bandage for his face.

And then the man's eyes *locked* on Lance's.

He grinned, exposing those awful, big blocky teeth.

Lance screamed and jumped as if he had been hooked up to jumper cables and given a good jolt. He was hysterical and kept screaming through hyperventilating gasps of air even as the man smiled even wider and then backed away quickly from the window. The man was screaming too but Lance could not understand it.

"...right *HERE*, Frankie! I've got the answer *RIGHT HERE*!

Lance was still screaming when the large window exploded toward him in a rainfall of glass shards. Lance was staring at the spot where the man's face had been and saw the shiny blade of a hatchet as it came through broadside and smashed the office window. The man had *slapped* the window with the hatchet on its side, rather than straight on with the blade.

The effect was an explosion of glass and startling noise.

The crashing sound of the window breaking snapped Lance out of his hysteria. He jumped up like a startled cat and seemed to *fly* away from the window. Lance actually *leaped* over the desk from a sitting position, something that he would never have been able to do under normal circumstances.

And, for the second time that night, Lance Davis ran for his life.

CHAPTER THIRTY

Margie's mood had soured.

Fully awake now and feeling much better after her nap, she had engaged her mind with busy-work around the house, became bored with it, and then progressed to a few guilty pleasures on the internet. Not even the celebrity gossip and some new pics of Brad Pitt could keep her mind from wandering back to Lance. She looked around the study and realized that the only light in the room was the illumination from the computer monitor.

Why are you sitting by yourself in the dark?

There was no immediate answer. During the web surfing session, Margie realized that she had crossed the threshold from irritation into full-fledged worry about Lance. She had considered calling the police, but balked when she had thought about what she would say.

Ma'am, you say you have a missing husband?

Yes, officer. He is a forty-two-year-old white male.

Ma'am, when did you last see him? It was about three-and-half hours ago when he went out to run some errands.

Uh huh. Yes, ma'am. So, let me get this straight. You think your forty-two-year-old husband is missing because he went out to run some errands and hasn't returned for three hours?

Well, three AND A HALF!

No traction there. That was a non-starter. Still, things weren't *right*. Even if Lance had decided to cut out and go with Carl drinking and carousing, he still would have called. He would have *called*. She knew her own husband, didn't she?

Don't I?

At the very least, Lance would have brought the hoses back to the house before he left. At the very least. The odd thing about it was that he was not in any condition to go out drinking again. He had come home drunk and sick, looking like hammered shit, and Margie knew that he had felt sick and tired all day. He had gotten almost no sleep. He would have hurried up to the store and come right back as soon as possible in the shape he was in.

None of this made sense.

Could he have had a heart attack or a stroke? Was he in the hospital? Her right hand moved up between her breasts and rested under her chin. She thought of Lance grabbing his chest and falling down inside *The Builder's Emporium.* Had someone seen it? Had someone *helped* him? Or maybe he had been in a car wreck. Was it possible that Lance had been flung through the windshield and was laying helpless out on an abandoned road somewhere? Surely someone would have found him; would have called an ambulance and made sure that he made it to a hospital.

Then why haven't they called me yet? They did that, didn't they? Didn't they call the family?

This last thought of Lance being in a car wreck was the most disturbing. Didn't that sort of thing happen all the time? Wasn't Lance a terrible driver? Always listening to the sports talk radio and getting so involved in the discussion that he yelled at it without paying attention to the road? Wasn't Lance always talking on the phone while driving?

He did all of these things.

Margie grabbed the phone book and sat down at the kitchen table near the only landline in the house. Lance had always wanted to get rid of it since they both had cell phones, but Margie liked having a *real* phone in the house. She also liked having a real, old fashioned, paper phonebook. She opened it to the "H" section and looked at the listings for hospitals. Only two major ones were listed, but there were several after-hours minor emergency clinics.

Okay, girl just hold on a sec. Get a grip. Isn't it more likely that your hubby is out with his friends rather than laid up in the hospital?

She looked down at the phone book. She got up and walked over to the junk drawer in the kitchen where she kept a stack of post-it notes (Lance called them "stickies"). She took one off the top, stuck it on the page where the hospital section started, and then closed the book. Lance was not in the hospital. She just felt that, wherever he had decided to go, he was not there.

She debated whether to call Carl Sanders.

She faced the fact that, instead of a heart attack or car wreck, it was more likely that Lance was with Carl somewhere, probably back out at *Cat Calls*, and had lost track of the time or was otherwise too *occupied* to call. That had to be it, or something close to it. But it was still odd that Lance had not called. She allowed him to go to places like that because she wanted him to be up front and honest about his whereabouts. It was just better that way. And it had worked. All these years it had worked.

But now, not so much.

She was loathe to call Carl. She did not like that sleazy pig, and only tolerated him at all because, for some weird reason, Lance liked the guy. Since Lance had to see him every day at work, Margie chose to not make any waves.

Even after *The Incident*.

The Incident had happened during the Christmas party last year at Frank Henderson's house. The party was pretty damn good, as they usually were at the Henderson house. A lot of people had shown up, in fact almost everyone from the office had been there, and the friends-of-friends who had appeared made the party even bigger and louder than usual. The food had been great and the booze had flowed like the Nile. Frank had actually hired a professional bartender to serve the liquor from an alcove set up in the backyard. As the hours had gone by and the later it had gotten, there were still a lot of people partying down.

Partying *hardy*.

Toward the end, most everyone had migrated outside by the pool. Several of the partygoers had stripped down to their skivvies and were actually in the water. As they watched to see who would be the first one to decide to go skinny-dipping, Margie had gone back inside to get another drink. In the kitchen were several people, one of whom was Carl, bleary-eyed and very drunk. Margie had pushed through the small crowd toward the fridge, opened it, and bent over to retrieve a coke.

As she had done so, she felt a hand on her ass.

Someone had grabbed her ass! She had looked back over her shoulder and there was Carl, grinning, holding a beer in his left hand and looking very proud of himself.

"Hey Margie, great party, huh?" Carl had said.

Margie was, for one of the few times in her life, flustered. Carl had not seemed to notice. He had moved his hand up from her ass, put his arm around her shoulder and proclaimed, "Margie, there might be guys who can drink *more* than me, but there ain't none that can get *drunker* than me!"

Carl and a few others within earshot had cackled at this bit of wit like it was the funniest thing they had ever heard. Margie had extricated herself from Carl's embrace, mumbled something in agreement and quickly went back outside.

He was just drunk, she had told herself.

Hell, he probably wouldn't even remember it in the morning. The nerve of the guy! Pawing at her when her own husband was right outside. He probably hadn't even known what he was doing.

But he *had* known.

Margie had seen Carl's eyes and *the look*. It was *the look* that men gave to women, and it made her very uncomfortable. He wasn't *that* drunk.

She had never mentioned it to Lance. Hadn't seen the point. She had just filed it away as *The Incident*.

Carl had never mentioned it either, thank goodness, but she had been avoiding him just the same ever since it had happened. But now it seemed she could think of no one else to call who might know where Lance was, other than maybe Frank. But she had already talked to Frank's wife, Jean, who had told her that Frank had never gone to work today because he was still nursing his hangover.

She picked up the landline and reluctantly dialed Carl's number. He answered on the first ring.

Of course he did.

"Hello? Lance?"

"Carl?" Margie inquired.

"Yeah, who is this? Margie?"

"Yes, Carl, this is Marge Davis. I was wondering if you know where Lance is."

She wanted to avoid chitchat.

"Margie! Hey, it's been a while," said Carl, sounding very surprised to receive a phone call from Margie.

"Yeah Carl, it has been, but I really need to speak to Lance. Have you seen him?"

"Nope. Haven't seen him since this morning at the office. But if he comes in, tell him to give me a call this weekend."

"Okay, Carl. Thanks. Buh-bye."

"Hey, Margie maybe we..."

Margie heard Carl trying to continue the conversation but she just hung up the phone. Even a few minutes with that pig was enough.

Margie frowned.

Although Carl could be lying and covering up for Lance, Margie didn't think so. He had sounded truly shocked when she called. Plus, there was no reason to get Carl to lie in the first place. Lance was a grown man. If he wanted to go out he would just tell her so that she wouldn't, well...*worry.*

Like she was doing now.

She looked at the phone book again, trying to decide what to do. In the end, she decided to wait a few more minutes to see if anyone or Lance himself called.

If not, then she would go out and look for her husband.

CHAPTER THIRTY-ONE

Over the crescendo of the broken window pane and the guttural sounds from the crazy man, Lance grunted as he vaulted over the desk in the little office and made a beeline to the door on the opposite wall. He had a fleeting, horrific thought that it would open into a closet, sealing his fate, but there was no turning back.

He was in a blind panic as he hurtled toward the door.

Walter had shattered the window and had jumped into the office with amazing quickness and agility. He had reached out and nearly grabbed Lance by the foot as Lance had leaped over the desk. Walter had not expected his quarry to be agile, and Walter's split-second of surprise is what saved Lance from being grabbed by the ankle in mid-leap and subsequently crashing unceremoniously on top of the desk.

Walter squeezed the rubber grip of the hatchet and leaped over the desk as well, right on Lance's heels.

Walter landed on the other side of the desk squarely on his left ankle, the same one that he had twisted earlier when he had landed on the board after Lance had repelled him from climbing up the lumber stacks. This time he landed on it awkwardly and it gave way under his weight. Walter sprawled on the floor face down right behind Lance as Lance tried to open the door.

Lance reached for the door knob, twisted it sharply, pulled the door open and, to his incredible relief, he saw that it opened into the back area of the store. As Lance ran toward this exit, he stepped forward and heard the man grunt with effort.

In the next instant Lance felt something hit hard against his right ankle.

Lance stutter-stepped once, his right foot coming down behind his left, and then was out of the office and into the back of the store. He ran four or five steps before it became apparent that something was wrong with his right ankle. It didn't seem to work any more. Lance thought that the man had slapped his foot, trying to trip him as they sometimes do in football games, but he saw the severity of the situation as he looked down at the back of his foot. It was numb, but he could see a deep gash there. It looked like the man had tried to cut off his foot from behind, but had only cut through the back third.

Lance winced as he stepped down on it and saw that the bone had been cut clean through. His ankle caved inward as he tried to walk on it.

He had been *hobbled*.

The hatchet, fucker hit me with it.

He looked around the back area. It was darker than the front but he could still see things well enough. He did not see a door or an exit sign. Worse, he saw nothing back here that he could use as a weapon. Lance cringed as he realized that all of the items that could be used as weapons were on the shelves out front. He had run away from them. He let out a sigh of despair.

Defenseless. I'm defenseless now. I can't even run.

In his panic, Lance looked around the area but all he saw were piles of lumber and bric-a-brac. Near him were some refrigerators and other large appliances still in boxes. He spied a box cutter tool with a retractable razor blade perched atop one of the boxed appliance units. Lance grabbed it instinctively. At best, he thought maybe he could hide, but quickly jettisoned that thought.

The crazy man would find him.

Lance took a step forward with an idea to run (*hobble*) to the front, get to a phone and maybe a knife from the case, and then take his chances–

Strong arms engulfed him from behind in a reverse bear hug, squeezing him close, pinning both arms to his sides, crushing the breath out of him, strong breath in his ear but no

*words, then release, the pressure abates from his chest for only
an instant, a huge intake of air, then a powerful arm moving up
from his chest to his neck, cradled in the V of an elbow, muscles
tense and flex, the arm pulls him hard, up and inward as it
burrows deep into his neck, his throat seems to collapse, fully
constricted as the arm squeezes and pulls him up and inward
from behind, the other arm coils at his right side, connects with
the arm that is choking him, locks into place, he feels a heavy
hand resting on the top of his head, pushing down as he is being
choked from behind and pulled up, lifted as his heels come off
the ground leaving the balls of his feet to support his weight as
the man deepens the choke upward and with greater force, no
oxygen at all, no sound, black dots bloom in his field of vision,
growing larger, there is no strength to break this hold, no
technique known to him that will cause release, the man is
behind him, shielded from attack, too strong*

Lance trained his concentration on his right hand, the one
holding the box cutter. He thumbed the blade out as far as it
would go, reached around to his left, and plunged the blade into
the only flesh that was available. He felt the blade sink into the
back of the maniac's tricep on the arm that was choking him.

No reaction.

Fading

Lance pulled the box cutter slowly toward him as he
pushed it into the arm. As it moved down the back of the man's
tricep, the razor sliced steadily through muscle and sinew about
an inch and a half deep, opening up a monstrous gash that

exposed the man's straining muscles. Lance continued pulling the blade along the man's arm as the razor did its work, rounded into the elbow and around to the soft forearm where Lance sliced in a line for about five full inches before the hold was broken.

The man bellowed in fury.

Lance collapsed to his knees, heaving great breaths into his oxygen-starved lungs.

He clutched the box cutter tightly in his right hand and tucked his chin into his chest in case the maniac tried to plant the choke again. Lance noticed grimly that his chin slid around on his chest that was now slippery with blood not his own.

Good

With his last remaining energy, Lance stood and hopped on one foot toward the narrow hall where the men's room was located, not bothering to turn and look at the man. Lance quickly assessed where he was. He could not return the way he had come, through the back-entrance door in the office, because he would have to go through the man. He thought that it was about an equal distance from where he was to the front of the store as it would be to double back to the office.

In the moment, he decided to head toward the front of the store if he could make it, to a telephone and the knife display where he would make his stand and take his chances. If he had to die while on the phone with 911 then so be it.

As he limped along he expected to be attacked from behind again so he kept his chin tucked into his chest and the box cutter at the ready. At the moment, he did not see anything that would make a better weapon.

As Lance hobbled along as fast as he could, he glanced around to see if the man was coming at him. If so, he might be forced to make a stand right there and then. Lance turned his head to look, but saw nothing. Nor could he hear anything.

As Lance passed the men's room door, he thought briefly about taking refuge in there, but decided against it. He did not recall if it had a lock, but even if it did he did not think that the crazy bastard would have much of a problem getting in. Lance was beyond half-assed measures at this point. He whimpered as he hopped as fast as he could into the back aisle. His lungs were on fire and he was out of breath.

He felt like he was quickly running out of *strength* as well.

For some reason, the maniac was not pursuing him but Lance knew that he would eventually, probably with some new horror planned for "Phoebe" or whatever it was that the man was seeing in Lance. Lance had to come up with a plan or a weapon to defend himself, but he was losing the thread.

Losing his *will*.

Lance had a stark realization that he was very likely going to die in this place.

The most frightening aspect of this realization was that he seemed to accept it on some level. Was almost resigned to it. This made him profoundly sad in a way that he could not fully rationalize. Had he given up? Was that possible?

Don't lose hope, old boy; stick around and fight. It ain't over 'til it's over.

Margie's worried face flashed in his mind, followed by the comically absurd idea that he might one day tell this story to Carl and Frank while getting shitfaced at *Cat Calls*.

Lance began to get angry.

What was it that his granddaddy had said? He had taken Lance to the cattle sales just south of Jackson. Lance always hated the smell, and the way that the big dumb animals were prodded around and treated, but he usually went because his granddaddy needed the help. As they had surveyed the stock from the catwalks, he'd nudged Lance and pointed. In one of the pens below, two bulls had squared off. One had been much larger than the other, but the smaller bull had not backed down. Lance had watched as the bigger bull had battered the smaller one. It had gone on until one of the hands had prodded them apart and then separated them into different pens. But through it all the smaller bull had never backed down.

His granddaddy had laughed, "Goddamn, that little sucker has some moxie." He had nudged Lance and said, "Bubba, do you know what you do when all ya got is a BB gun?"

"No, sir."

"You fire your BBs, son."

"You fire your fucking BBs, that's what," Lance mumbled as he used the last of his resolve to shuffle down the aisle toward the front of the store.

As he headed toward a center island with a large banner hanging overhead that proclaimed PAINT DEPARTMENT LET US MIX WHILE YOU SHOP! he saw further up the large glass display case containing the assortment of knives.

When it came down to it, he wanted to have a little bit better than a BB gun.

CHAPTER THIRTY-TWO

Tommy Jones sat on his couch in his small apartment watching one of his favorite movies, *Under Siege 2: Dark Territory*. Although he did not much care for Seagal, he liked this movie (and also the first one) because the villains were far more interesting than the hero. Tommy watched as the mercenary Marcus Penn (as far as Tommy was concerned, Everett McGill was a great actor) walked along the railroad tracks, looked down and picked up the all-important CD.

Marcus examined it before delivering one of Tommy's favorite movie lines: "Chance favors the prepared mind."

"Damn straight it does," answered Tommy.

He picked up his cell and keyed in Harvey.

"Any word on Walter?" Tommy asked.

"No."

"What does Harmon think?"

"That maybe he went on to Jackson where he's from. Nowhere for a guy like that to go around here."

"Yeah, but that don't make no sense. I was going to take him to Jackson. That's what I don't understand. Why would he just bug out like that? Don't make no sense."

Harvey did not respond.

Tommy broke the silence.

"What's the plan?"

"Nothing proactive, although Harmon did send me to check out the *Emporium*, thinking maybe that he went there because of...you know. I drove by it about an hour ago and it was closed. Locked up tight. Harmon says to let the staties handle it."

"OK. Let me know if you hear anything." Tommy ended the call.

Tommy continued to watch the movie without really watching it. He was trying to think of some way to unfuck this situation. Walter had burned him. Had in fact *exposed* him to the possibility of official inquiry into his conduct. Tommy still did not know what kind of game Walter was playing, and did not really think that it involved him personally, but still, the thing was...Walter would eventually get caught.

They *always* got caught–especially the crazy ones.

What would Walter say when they caught him? *That* was

what concerned Tommy. Walter had always been cool. They had had an understanding. Although Tommy trusted no one, he had somehow failed to see Walter's motivations. He'd gotten sloppy or lazy at some point over the last four years. He tried to think back to what he had missed, but he could not see it.

Tommy turned off the television.

Walter was high profile. Every state trooper and local flatfoot in the area would be on alert. But none of them wanted to find Walter worse than Tommy. Walter was a loose end. An extreme liability. Tommy was going to have to take care of things himself. He got dressed. The last thing he did was strap on his service piece, a Glock 9mm.

Tommy lived alone. Lived frugally in a small apartment. He did not believe in spending money on extravagance when it could be spent on much better things. He drew open the curtain in the living room and looked outside. His apartment was not exactly in the nicest neighborhood. No suburban cul-de-sac for Tommy. He preferred to be closer to the action. He looked out the window toward *The Builder's Emporium* just five blocks away.

He had told Harmon to check out the *Emporium*. Harmon had said that he would, but for Tommy to go home for the time being. Harmon had his suspicions about Tommy and Walter. He had chosen to just send Tommy home rather than suspend him. Harmon had said that he wanted to think things through, which meant that he wanted more time to dig around for dirt on Tommy.

Although Harvey had said that he had checked out the *Emporium*, Tommy was skeptical. Harvey had most likely just phoned that in. He probably did not even get out of his car.

The scanner traffic had been heavy all day as a result of Walter's little escapade. Both the local police and the county Sheriff had checked with the manager at the *Emporium* and there had been no problems there. As Harvey had said, it was closed and locked down tight.

Still, Tommy might take a walk over that way and see what he could see. As far as he knew there was no one staked out at the *Emporium*, although the shrink and the lawyer had requested some security and had received it. Tommy could only wish that Walter would show up at his apartment wanting to try some of his crazy shit. That would be a godsend. Tommy had observed Walter for over four years. He was sure Walter was still in the area, most likely in the vicinity of the *Emporium* although he told this to no one. He had no evidence, just a hunch.

But it was a strong one.

He had no jurisdiction to do anything outside of the Hill, but he could still legally carry a firearm as a former peace officer; and, of course, as a concerned citizen there was no law that said that he could not check things out.

Tommy double-checked his weapon, holstered it, and walked out of his apartment.

CHAPTER THIRTY-THREE

Walter was still in the back.

He was not in real good shape, but felt well enough to finish the job. He had re-injured his ankle when he had jumped over the desk and landed on the floor, but he had been able to inflict a little damage himself with the hatchet. Walter didn't think that the Frankie-thing could climb back up the lumber stacks with an ankle that looked like that. If it could, then Walter might have to take the fight up there, which could prove difficult.

Walter's left arm was shredded. He had tried to hold onto the choke long enough to end things, and he had nearly succeeded until that nasty stinger had come out of nowhere.

As much as his arm had spurted colors into his head, and as bad as it looked, he could still use it. Walter had found a roll of duct tape and simply wrapped his arm with it to stop the bleeding and to close the wound. It was a stop-gap measure, but it would do for now.

It had not taken Walter long to wrap his arm. He had watched the Frankie-thing limp away and understood that it had very little fight left. It was going nowhere. Walter wanted to take his time now and enjoy his triumph. After he had finished wrapping his arm he had started to walk toward the front of the store in pursuit, intending to attack again. But this time he would fully disarm it and tie it up before proceeding with the cleansing. It would be much safer that way.

Walter limped along the way that

Frankie? Phoebe?

had gone, pursuing it, but stopped when something caught his attention.

It was on a shelf, out of the box for some reason, right above the storage closets where the lawnmowers and trimmers were kept.

Walter's ankle had begun to swell, but he ignored the pain-color signals that it sent to his brain and stretched upward, on his tippy-toes, until he grabbed it off the shelf. He had to make sure that it worked.

If it did, his work here would be complete in a very short time.

CHAPTER THIRTY-FOUR

Margie pulled out of the driveway and drove toward *Cat Calls* to try to find Lance. He was still not answering his cell and he was not at the office. She was running out of ideas. As much as she loathed going there, the upscale titty bar was the only place she could think of to look.

If he *was* there, then she was–as Chet liked to say– definitely going to get up into his shit.

She pulled out of a side street in her neighborhood and onto the busy main highway that would take her to *Cat Calls*. As she drove, she realized that *The Builder's Emporium* was on the way.

Might as well.

She decided to slow down and check it out. There was no other traffic behind her so she was able to slow down almost to a stop in the roadway as she came upon the *Emporium*. As she coasted, Margie looked to her right at the huge front parking lot which appeared to be roped off for some reason. It was mostly empty and the store looked closed. Still, she decided to pull in and check it out.

Just to make sure.

She drove by the front doors and saw that it was, in fact, closed. Lance was not there.

If he doesn't show up tonight she would tell the police to question the employees there to try and pinpoint the last time that someone had seen him. She might even do that herself. Maybe one of them would recognize...

Lance's car.

Margie stomped on the brakes. She wheeled around in a looping u-turn and drove to the other end of the parking lot which merged into the bustling lot of *Pepe's Pizza*. The lot at *Pepe's* abutted the *Emporium's* and it looked like several of *Pepe's* customers had parked in the *Emporium's* spaces.

Lance's Mercury Marquis was parked there as well.

Margie pulled in next to the Marquis to make sure. Her heart sped up a little and her hands were sweating. She tried to remain calm, but the nervousness would not abate. Margie parked next to the Marquis and got out of her car. She looked at the license plate first. She then realized that she had never bothered to memorize the tag number and did not know if this was Lance's car or not. She proceeded further on and looked in through the window of the driver's side door. Margie cupped her hands around her face and, with the aid of the street light nearby, was able to see Lance's dry cleaning lying on the passenger side seat.

What *looked* like his dry cleaning at any rate. She raced around to the passenger side to get a better look at the ticket stapled at the top of the hangers. She was sure the shirts were Lance's, or at least were like the ones that he wore, but confirmed it when she was able to make out the "L" as the first letter of the customer's name on the ticket.

This *was* Lance's car.

Why was it here? Where was he?

She stood still, hands on hips, and looked over at *The Builder's Emporium*. It was obviously closed. She walked toward the front door of *Pepe's*, up the sidewalk and past a man who was standing outside smoking a cigarette and looking a little too closely at her chest as she walked by. Margie went inside. She walked quickly around the interior, canvassed the diners, and circled back to the front door.

No Lance.

She walked back outside, ignoring the smoking man, and stood still with indecision. Her gaze was drawn again to the *Emporium*. That was where he had gone. If he had parked his car there and then went inside, why hadn't he come back out? Had someone picked him up here? Was he still inside, injured as she had feared earlier at the house?

Margie was scared. She decided to walk in the direction of the *Emporium*. It was about a hundred yards to the front doors, which looked sealed with heavy metal burglar guards, but she walked in that direction anyway, hoping to find some sort of clue.

CHAPTER THIRTY-FIVE

Lance was hunched over at the end of the long aisle, near the checkout stations and the paint center. He had tried the phone at the station. The line was dead. He had tried another phone at another station. It was also dead. He could see the cords running up a long pipe and into the ceiling. They did not appear to have been cut or disconnected, but the man must have done something to them because none of them seemed to work.

Lance felt like crying.

Felt the *hope* draining from him. There was not going to be any help. He was left to his own devices. To his *fate*.

Blood dripped from his right hand.

After the demoralizing check on the operation of the

phones, Lance had taken the red rag off his injured left hand finger and wrapped it around his right hand. He then proceeded to use his right hand to smash the glass display case that covered the cache of knives. Even with the rag, he had managed to cut himself.

Lance collapsed amid the checkout stations in a sitting position with his legs splayed out in front of him, trying to apply pressure to the newest cut on his right hand. In his lap was the prize from the knife case–a large and very sharp hunting knife.

It looked like a murder weapon.

Lance had felt like an idiot the moment that his hand had hit the case. As the case had shattered, he had felt the sharp, piercing sting of a large sliver of glass.

Hey sport, this is your hand talking here. Yeah, the right one. Say, did you happen to notice that there are about a million objects in this fucking store that you could have used to break the glass? You know, other than your hand? I know I'm not the brains of this outfit, but next time try not to be such a dumbshit. Mmmkay?

Focus.

Once the glass had shattered, Lance had panicked once again when he saw that the knives were tied down to the display rack with what seemed like unbreakable plastic. Like they had broken the law and had been cuffed by the knife-police with tiny plastic handcuffs.

He needed, well…*a fucking knife* to cut them so he could access the knives.

There was still no sign of the maniac.

Whatever he was doing, he was being quiet for the time being but Lance knew that would not last long. Lance had hobbled around the corner and grabbed the closest thing available which had turned out to be a large tree saw, the kind that had the blade with the large triangular teeth suspended by a "J"-shaped piece of metal. Lance had used the saw to cut the plastic band and obtain the hunting knife.

It was his last line of defense.

If this did not work, Lance was resigned to his fate.

After he had acquired the hunting knife, Lance had collapsed on the floor with the knife in his hand and the branch saw by his side. He slid the saw along the cement floor behind the checkout counter.

He was fading fast.

He had re-opened the wound on his left hand but could not remember how it had happened. He thought that maybe he had smacked it against the desk in the little office when the maniac had scared the shit out of him and made him jump.

In addition to that, his right hand appeared to be cut more deeply than he had initially thought. Not that it mattered. His bleeding hands were the least of his problems.

His ankle was in the most serious shape of all. It was still, mercifully, numb (for the most part), but Lance could see–and *feel*–that he was injuring himself more each time he tried to walk on it. He collapsed to take his weight off it.

It was grinding bone on bone with each step he took.

He wanted desperately to climb back up to the top of the lumber stacks and fight from the high ground. That might afford him a chance. Maybe not a good chance, but certainly better than what he faced now. He might have even tried it with his mangled hands, but the ankle was too severely injured. He could barely walk on it and climbing would be impossible. The stacks were so far away that he doubted he could make it over there in the first place–even if he hopped on one foot–much less climb the support beams if he did. He had doubts whether he would be able to walk again even if he survived this ordeal.

Lance shuddered.

It was a full-body, involuntarily shake, similar to the muscle-quivers that followed the first few times he had tried beer or strong whiskey, only much more pronounced. Lance felt himself going into shock for real and there was nothing that he could do about it.

He needed medical attention.

All of a sudden he was thirsty and hungry. He was also cold. He felt a feeling of *urgency*. This thing had to end soon or his body was simply going to shut down and slip into unconsciousness. If that happened he would no doubt–*hardy har har*–wake up and find himself dead.

Probably in *pieces*.

He had sprung a million leaks. Pain registered from every quadrant of his body. But as Lance sat bunkered down behind the checkout station, he grasped that the real killer was the dehydration.

He had not been able to drink anything since…he could not remember. It had been a long time ago.

Just before he mowed the lawn?

That seemed like so long ago. He had wounds that bled, had the bout of diarrhea, and had to fight the fever from the bad fish. The fever was back. His forehead was hot and dry. His throat was swollen from being crushed by the choke hold, and his mouth was so dry that he could not summon any spittle at all.

Part of him almost wished that he had not fought the maniac in the back part of the store when he had had the choke hold sunk in. He could have just not resisted it and passed on into silent oblivion. Saved himself some agony and what was shaping up to be a nasty death.

His thinking was muddled and he found it difficult to concentrate.

Lance propped himself up against the checkout station so that he was facing the way that he had come. Directly down the aisle in front of him was the narrow hall that led into the back of the store. The aisle was very long, probably fifty yards or so.

Lance trained his eyes on it for any sign of the maniac. Nothing.

Lance mulled over the irony of the situation. It was torture making him sit and wait like this. The fucker had terrorized him by chasing him all over the store, but now was terrorizing him more by doing nothing.

Stay alert, pal. The family is coming over tomorrow and you can't miss it. Don't forget about that.

Lance smiled a little at that one. He had come here, after all, to purchase two water hoses. What were the odds of something like this happening? He backtracked in his mind to the string of events that had to occur in order to place him in this situation. It was a string of *ifs*.

If he hadn't gone out with Carl and Frank, and *if* the fucking chef had not served him bad fish, and *if* the lovely "Stormy" and her friends at *Cat Calls* had tits like Alley McBeal's instead of Anna Nicole Smith's, and *if* he hadn't *run over* the fucking garden hose with the fucking lawnmower, and the entire host of other *ifs* that had to occur in order for him to be lying here with a sliced ankle, two bleeding hands, a fucking *nail* wound through his finger and calf, on queer street from being choked almost into unconsciousness, and now waiting to be attacked by some crazy bastard for no apparent reason.

The perfect alignment of circumstance was unbelievable. It also wasn't fair. What were the odds that he would end up like this from just trying to buy some garden hoses?

The odds? The odds you say? Bucko, I got the answer right here. The odds are exactly 100%.

Because here he was.

But you know it could have been Margie.

Lance froze, stunned by this hideous thought.

He slowly let out a jet of tepid breath through his dry mouth and tried to let that mental image sink in.

That's right, pardner. Margie could have said, okay, hon, I'll just go up to the store and get the hoses, you just finish mowing the lawn and then go in and take a nap. I'll be right back. Shit, he would still be sleeping while she was here...Yeah, but she wouldn't have stayed in the head and missed the store closing announcement, and let's not forget, t'ain't likely that Margie would shit on her own hand, drop her cell phone, and break it for Christ's sake. But how do you know he would have waited if he saw her? He is looking for someone called Phoebe. You see, pardner, it could just as easily have been Margie lying where you are now. Have a nice day!

That was cruel.

Lance felt pangs of rage begin to boil inside of him. Because the voice was right. It *could* have easily been his Margie lying here injured or...worse. Much worse. He did not want to think such black thoughts, but found that he was unable to *not* think them. Worst of all was the image of Margie ending up like that other girl (*Amy? Amanda?*) who was killed right inside this store, probably by the same psychotic that was trying to kill him now.

Lance remembered when it had happened.

His mind edged toward an emotional abyss.

Sliding into shock now, he clung to that unspeakable thought to give himself strength. He was near the end of his endurance again, but this time he was sure that there was no more juice left in the batteries. If he went down this time that was it. He would be down for the proverbial count.

He needed all the strength that he could muster. Right now he found that the easiest way–maybe the *only* way–to get there was to allow himself to be immersed in the most primal emotion of them all.

Just as the silence of the *The Builder's Emporium* was cataclysmically shattered by the object the maniac was holding above his head as he limped from the narrow hallway toward the figure lying against the checkout station, Lance Davis's emotional throttle kicked into overdrive as anger turned swiftly into red rage.

This was *it*.

CHAPTER THIRTY-SIX

Tommy Jones had been loitering around *Pepe's Pizza* for about an hour with nothing to show for it other than a full stomach and an even nastier disposition than when he had arrived. He sat in a booth drinking his fourth cup of coffee. The remains of his spaghetti and meatball dinner had been cleaned off a half hour ago. He had chosen the booth because of the view. Outside of the bay window he could see *The Builder's Emporium.*

It looked dark and quiet at the moment.

His instincts had led him here, but now he felt stymied.

The waitress walked by and gave him the eye. She offered some more coffee but in a manner that indicated that she would much rather pour the hot coffee down his pants rather than in his empty cup. Tommy did not blame her.

"That's all right, darlin', I'm leavin'," Tommy said.

The waitress pulled back the carafe, nodded and walked on to the next table.

He would at least leave a good tip. Although he lived close to *Pepe's* he rarely ate there. There was something about a pizza place with a Mexican name that he did not fully trust. He might have to reevaluate after tonight though, since Pepe outdid himself on the meatballs. The meal had been very good. He wished he was in a better mood to enjoy it.

Tommy checked in with Harvey one more time.

Nada.

Tommy paid the bill and walked out of *Pepe's* into the night air. It was still hot and humid. He stood outside and breathed deeply before fishing a Marlboro out of a pack and lighting up. There were a few kids in the parking lot drinking and talking. They did not seem to notice Tommy and he paid no attention to them. As he took another drag, he saw a woman drive by slowly in the lot and then stop beside a Marquis that was parked in *Pepe's* lot, but in the farthest possible spot that was close to the front of the *Emporium*.

Tommy watched as she exited her car and tried the door on the Marquis. Locked. She then pressed her face to the window on one side and then the other, obviously looking for something important. She seemed excited.

She was also *very* attractive.

Tommy crushed out his smoke and watched the woman. She looked like she had gotten dressed and left her house in a hurry. Her hair was pinned up in a ball on top of her head, she had on sweat pants and tennis shoes and what appeared to be only a men's white t-shirt with no bra. Tommy surveilled her chest movements and concluded that her full titties were swinging free underneath the cotton.

Tommy perked up. This was worth another smoke which he lit as he watched the woman.

As she peered again into the backseat of the car, she seemed to find what she was looking for and relaxed a little bit before turning toward him.

No. Not relaxed.

What she had seen in the car had worried her even more. As she strode toward him he was suddenly self-conscious about staring at her tits. She appeared to be on her way to confront him about it. Tommy Jones was feeling a little bit embarrassed for the first time in a great many years, not that he owed her an explanation for staring nor would he give her one. The embarrassment turned into amusement however as she walked right past him and into *Pepe's*.

Ah well.

Tommy took a final toke on his cigarette and crushed it out on the sidewalk. He had taken a step to walk back to his apartment when the doors to *Pepe's* flew open and the same attractive woman walked out, strode right past him again, and stopped at her car.

She put her hands on her hips and stood still for a moment, looking directly at the *Emporium*.

Studying it.

Tommy was curious. He made no pretense about staring at the woman. She did not appear to notice him. Tommy was taken aback when she started walking directly to the front doors of the *Emporium*, which stood dark and covered by metal security doors. The place was obviously not open for business.

Yet onward she went.

Tommy felt a pang of...*something*. It was that cop-sense that told him that something was going on here and he had better pay attention. It was the same intuition that had kept him out of trouble all his life. It alerted him to danger and he did not ignore it now. During his years in uniform, before he became a babysitter in the nuthouse, that feeling would tell him that, on this particular traffic stop, he should call for backup; or on that particular raid, he should not take the point; or on this particular call, he should make sure the house is clear.

His cop-sense told him to follow the woman.

Tommy trailed after her, keeping a safe distance. The woman walked with purpose to the front doors of the *Emporium*. As she did, Tommy could not help noticing the way her ass moved under the sweat pants. He did his best to ignore it. That was just the sort of thing that short-circuited good police sense and ended up with things in a fucked up mess.

She was almost to the front doors.

Tommy walked out of the parking lot at an angle, toward

the corner of the *Emporium* so he could observe her from the side and walk against the building for some cover. He reached around to the small of his back to make sure that his Glock was ready in case he needed it.

It had no safety.

The woman stopped at the front doors.

She put her hands on the doors and tried to peer inside like she did with the car. She did this for a while and then placed her ear to the doors, trying to listen for something inside the store. She did this for an uncomfortably long time before finally stepping back and saying something.

Tommy walked a little closer to the woman to hear what she was saying. It was a man's name. She said it several times, each louder than the last.

She was yelling for someone named Lance.

CHAPTER THIRTY-SEVEN

Walter limped along the back of the store.

He rounded the corner to the entrance of the narrow hallway that led past the men's room and then out into the main part of the store. He held the object that he had taken down from the shelf tightly in his left hand. His hand worked just fine, but his left arm was feeling strange. Blood and fluid were seeping from the sliced skin through the duct tape, but the tape held fast, giving his arm a surprising amount of support. With his right hand, Walter pulled the cord and, on the second try, the chainsaw roared to life inside the narrow hallway.

The sound was deafening.

Walter revved it up as loud as it would go and loped toward the prone figure lying on the floor near one of the checkout stations. Walter trudged along steadily with the screaming chainsaw held out in front of him almost to shoulder height.

His limp was pronounced, but he moved with purpose.

Walter had lost any concept of being locked up again at Spring Hill. He had been able to climb the grids of his mind one last time, but had somehow fallen in a way that he could not express. He had the sensation in his mind of falling and falling, never stopping, never hitting bottom; nor did he want to stop.

The pain in his head went away as he fell and he embraced it. As he fell from the grids he saw the lattice-work that he had created over so many years fade away above him, and with it the last chance he would ever have at sanity.

As Walter approached the figure lying next to one of the checkout stations, he sensed fear. The figure appeared to Walter as an indiscriminate being, alternately a grotesque form of the person he had known as Phoebe, then Frankie from his childhood so long ago, then as a scorpion-thing that hissed with fear and showed its stinger. The vision in Walter's right eye was fading. Only a fraction of the sensory input from his eyes was reaching his brain at this point as the tumor ravaged and plundered.

Over the roar of the chainsaw, which he barely heard, Walter perceived that the figure was now a man. Closer now, Walter saw that the figure clutched a large hunting knife and looked angry, but it was evident that he was injured and weak.

Walter would make it quick.

He imagined that slaying the man would free him–relieve the *pressure* in his head–and that a whole new world would await him on the outside. His head would be normal again. His *mind*. No more heaviness. No more headaches or confusion. No more reason to be afraid every time he went to sleep.

Yes, he would have to do this quickly, but *thoroughly*.

And then by God, *he could spread his wings and fly!*

Walter picked up the pace and, with the chainsaw rumbling he closed the distance. As he got closer, he noticed that the man threw the knife aside, grabbed something from his lap and simply tossed it toward Walter.

Walter realized what it was immediately, but had no idea why the man would throw it at him until it was too late.

CHAPTER THIRTY-EIGHT

Come on you son of a bitch! Get closer. That's right.
Up close and personal.

Lance could see the hideous look of triumph on the maniac's face as he trudged forward faster and faster with the chainsaw throttled full bore. This was all the confirmation Lance needed in order to steel himself for what he intended to do. He had a brief moment of doubt where he thought he might hesitate when it truly counted and fall prey to the tortured delusions of this troubled man. But, from the looks of things, it appeared that this maniac intended to cut up Lance with a chainsaw. That changed things considerably, but Lance was still glad that he had been able to see the crazy man's face.

The *resolve* there. The look in his eyes. In them, Lance saw that whatever this man had once been was now gone. Lance was not even sure if the man could see him in a rational way, but it was evident that he was not going to stop. Lance took comfort in this and braced himself for what had to be done.

Lance continued to watch the maniac's face as he tossed aside the hunting knife and grabbed the book of matches that he had purloined from Randy Philpot's office.

As the man made his final approach toward Lance, the roar of the chainsaw drowned out the sound of the paint thinner leaking out of the punctured cans that lined the middle of the aisle. They were lined up neatly in rows on the shelves. Over fifty of them leaked prodigious amounts of the highly flammable paint thinner from the holes put there by Lance. He had used the box cutter blade as he had limped down the aisle earlier, piercing the cans twice to aerate them so the liquid would flow out in a smooth stream.

The crazed man with the chainsaw followed the path.

Lance had a feeling of close to pure ecstasy as he saw the dawning realization on the maniac's face that he was now standing in a rather large puddle of paint thinner, and that Lance held a fully lit book of matches in his hand. Lance had lit one of the matches and then placed it next to all the others, igniting the whole book at once to create a large flame.

Lance tossed the flaming book of matches at the thin tendril of paint thinner that had flowed in his direction to within three feet of his leg.

Even as the flaming matchbook was in the air, Lance rolled around the corner and ducked under the shelter of the cosest checkout station. Lance heard a

WWWWWHHOOOOOOOOOOOOOOSSSSHHHH!!!

sound as if the building itself had sucked in a deep breath. The sound of the chainsaw was drowned out by the explosion that followed, as were the higher-pitched sounds made by the man's outraged screams as the fire ate into his skin.

Lance covered his ears.

CHAPTER THIRTY-NINE

Margie pressed her ear to the front door of the *Emporium* and listened. She could hear the shrill whine of a small motor of some sort, but no voices. She pressed again, harder this time. Still nothing.

But she *had* heard voices in there.

Well, of course, there are voices in there. That's because it's a really big store, and really big stores have these things called "employees" who take care of things inside said store, and sometimes these so-called "employees" have to say things to each other

She silenced the sarcasm. Of course they were store employees. Had to be. But they were yelling. *Screaming* at each other, in fact. Otherwise she would not have been able to hear them over the din of

a leaf blower? weedeater?

whatever it was making the noise. One of the voices was far away, but getting closer. The other was close to the front where she listened.

It was the voice at the front that sounded like

"Lance?" Margie said as she took a step back and addressed the closed front doors of the *Emporium*.

Take it easy.

It sounded a little bit like him, but lots of guys probably would when they talked loudly and through a security door. There was no way to be sure.

But it sounds like he is screaming in there.

"Lance?!" said Margie. "Are you in there? Answer me if you are!"

No answer from within. From the periphery of her field of vision she noticed that the smoker at *Pepe's* had followed her here and seemed to be getting closer.

"LANCE! ARE YOU IN THERE?!" Margie screamed at the front door. She was on the verge of tears.

Margie turned to look at the smoker. While she had been absorbed with locating (*Lance?*) he had walked up close to her, probably to within twenty or thirty feet, but he still kept a respectable distance.

Although she was a little bit apprehensive about his approach, his manner was not threatening. As she watched him come closer she could see that he was not menacing at all. He was...*curious*.

"Who do you think is in there?"

Margie slumped. He saw that she was frightened, but not of him. She still looked beautiful, even more so the closer he came, but now he saw that she was *fatigued*. She was unsure of what to do or say. She just needed a little push.

"Who do you think is in there?" His voice was pleasant and even.

She looked at him, trying to decide what to do. There was a long, silent pause before she spoke.

"My husband."

The words hung in the air for a moment. Tommy Jones could see that she was deciding whether to just spill it to a stranger. His sense was that she would, and his police-sense told him to just be quiet and wait for it. He could tell she was frightened and wanted to talk about it.

They *always* wanted to talk about it.

Tommy was about twenty feet away, walking slowly along the storefront toward the woman. She stood directly in front of the main entrance. She took a deep breath. That was a good sign. Tommy said nothing.

Wait for it...Wait for it.

"I think...I think I heard my husband in there."

She was near tears.

Tommy saw that since she had spilled some of it, she had decided to spill it all. This was how it usually happened.

Tommy considered the situation. Several things had now become obvious. She was married. Her husband's name was Lance. He drove a Mercury Marquis. The Marquis had been parked out by *Pepe's* for a long time. She did not know where her husband was. He was obviously *not* an employee at the store. She thought he was inside. And for some reason–the *real* reason that Tommy was now intrigued–ol' Lance was apparently unable to communicate with her, even though he was presumably inside the *Emporium*.

Why would that be? Why couldn't he just come out?

"That Marquis is Lance's car, isn't it?"

"*Yes!*" said the woman, surprised that he knew this.

That's right, sugar, just let it out. Tell ol' Tommy all about it.

"He came up here to buy some garden hoses *hours* ago and hasn't come home!" she cried.

The dam had burst and she went on, talking very fast.

"He didn't call or answer his cell. And now his car is here but there is no sign of him. He would have *called* me. There is no reason why he would just drive up here and then disappear like…"

BOOOOOOOOOOOOOOOOOOOOOM!!!

The main entrance of the store seemed to expand for a moment before Tommy's eyes, followed by an explosion and a low, rolling shock wave that came through the front of the *Emporium*. The woman was cut off in mid-sentence. Tommy saw her levitate as the wave lifted her off the ground a few feet and then pushed her backwards onto the pavement about ten feet into the parking lot. He noticed that in her surprise and flight she had the awareness to wrap her hands around her head as she flew through the air, protecting her head from impact with the pavement when gravity eventually took over again.

Tommy sensed small objects flying through the air in front of him (*glass? nails?*) but he was unaffected by the blast wave.

He ran to the woman.

She had landed hard on the pavement but appeared to be okay. Tommy knelt and told her to stay down and stay still, but she tried to sit up anyway. She was dazed. Pieces of glass and other debris were sprinkled in her hair and on her clothing. Tommy noticed a long and wicked looking scrape that ran down the back of her left hand all the way to her elbow where it had skidded along the pavement. Tommy was amazed that she had had the instinct to cradle her head with her left arm as she flew through the air. Although it resulted in a nasty scrape along her left arm, the maneuver had likely prevented serious injury to her head.

Smart girl.

"Are you okay?" Tommy asked. It was difficult for him to tell if she had sustained any serious injuries. Tommy thought she must have a concussion or possibly a broken bone somewhere.

"Lance," she said in a thick drawl. She tried to sit up on her own but could not manage it.

He held her steady and helped her sit up as she tried to get her bearings. They both looked back at the *Emporium*. Tommy saw that the explosion was localized. The entire building had not blown up, only a small section near the front.

The metal roll-down security covers over the main doors were still hinged top and bottom, but had bent outward from the force of the blast, like angry gray sails that had tried to defy the wind but had bent nonetheless. Tommy saw that the metal security covers had saved the woman. They had borne the brunt of the blast, although the shock wave had still come through on the right-hand side, blasting a partition through the space where the door joined the wall. Through it, Tommy could see inside the store a little bit.

He could see fire.

If the woman had heard voices, then it meant there were people inside.

Tommy stood and started to walk toward the front doors. As he did so, the woman grabbed his hand with both of hers and pulled herself to her feet. Tommy said nothing and simply allowed her to use his arm to steady herself. She followed behind him, holding on to his arm as he walked toward the *Emporium*.

They walked in this manner toward the opening that had been created by the blast. It appeared to be big enough for a man to slide through, but it would be tight.

Tommy approached with caution, cognizant of the possibility that another, more powerful explosion might be waiting for them. If so, they would be walking right into it.

Tommy was on alert. In situations like this, there was danger *everywhere.*

He considered just retreating and calling 911. Let them deal with it. But the woman pushed him onward, crushing her breasts into his arm and side, followed by the full weight of her body as she leaned into him, directing him toward the now-smoking front doors of the *Emporium.* Although Tommy could have easily resisted her efforts, he did not do so. He allowed himself to be moved that way. If there were people in there, they most likely needed some immediate attention, and he was trained to provide at least some rudimentary first aid.

There was something else.

As Tommy and Margie approached, screams and angry yelling echoed from inside underneath a cacophonous buzzing caused by some unidentified gas-powered engine. The voices were engaged in a back and forth exchange that was not quieted by the explosion, but rather seemed to have been enhanced *because* of it. It was two men.

They were close.

And they were *raging*.

"*LANCE!*" Margie screamed.

She let go of Tommy's arm and took a few clumsy steps toward the recently formed, jagged entrance into the *Emporium.* Tommy made no effort to stop her. He watched as she ambled to within five feet or so of the entryway, intent on going inside to assist Lance.

But before she could make it through, she stopped, wobbled, lost her balance, and then stutter-stepped backward for ten feet before plopping down squarely on her ass, like a giant toddler who had taken several big steps, but then discovered that this walking thing was not as easy as it looked. She tried to get up again for another try but was having trouble doing so.

Tommy ignored her and looked at the entryway.

He had already drawn his Glock and cradled it in his hands at the ready position, trigger-finger off the guard and parallel with the barrel. He tried to concentrate through the adrenaline jolt that coursed through his body, focusing on controlling the weapon in his hands and making sure that his steps were measured and sure. As he approached the entryway, he could feel the heat of the fire inside, but there was no live fire directly blocking his way in.

Tommy squeezed through the hole and into the *Emporium.*

The woman had apparently recognized one of the voices as the wayward Lance. Tommy did not know if that voice belonged to Lance or not.

But he sure as shit recognized the other voice.

CHAPTER FORTY

Assistant Manger Randy Philpot was at his apartment trying to unwind.

He lived alone and had no girlfriend at the moment, although he had always thought that the little checkout girl, Heidi, had a nice rack. He had given some thought to trying to bag that, but figured that it would not be worth it if he had to actually have a conversation with her. They had been in the break room a few weeks ago and Randy had mentioned something about Malcolm X. Neither Heidi nor Cheryl had known who he was. Randy could not believe it. He thought they were joking.

Nope.

Plus, Randy got the feeling that they talked about him behind his back. But really, what else could one expect when there were three and sometimes six teenaged girls in one place. It was a natural law of the universe. Still, Heidi pushed his buttons. There was no law that required him to stick around for *conversation*, was there?

Randy was splayed out on his couch, remote control in one hand, trying to get in the mood. He flipped through the considerable selection of satellite porn available to him on the television. Several movies were already in progress, but Randy opted for a fresh one. He was intrigued by the Academy Award winning *Junk In Da Trunk VII*, which was mere moments away from starting.

Randy was almost *fully* in the mood when his home phone rang.

Like the Davises, Randy was of a generation that had grown up with a landline. He liked having a landline in addition to his cell, even though he rarely used it. It was rarer still that someone called him on it. He had no friends (no *real* friends, anyway), and his family hardly ever called. When someone did, it usually meant something serious.

He answered it immediately.

"Mr. Randy Philpot?" It was an official sounding woman's voice.

"Yes?" Randy replied.

"This is the 911 emergency system."

She explained to him that the fire alarm at *The Builder's*

Emporium had been activated, and that they had also received a call from someone at *Pepe's Pizza* who had reported seeing an explosion and possibly a fire in the store. Randy was the primary contact they had listed for store management. She asked if he would meet the firemen at the store and allow them entry if needed.

He said he would.

Oh fuck me!

Talk about a boner deflater. Randy reached for his jeans as his mind raced in a panic. He tried to recall how he had left the store. If this was somehow his fault, he was *fucked*.

A *fire*?

A fucking *explosion*?

How could that be? The place had been shut down properly. He had seen to it personally. He had locked up just like he always did. He had double-checked everything. He was not in charge of anything that could have resulted in an *explosion*. It had to be one of those nimrod checkout girls. One of them had probably left a cigarette going or some other shittin'-ass thing.

He could not believe it.

Maybe Purvis Cooper had been careless about something in the back. He was always trying to impress the checkout girls with his stories about the Nail Gun Killer. Purvis was not one who paid attention to detail. If it was up to Randy he would fire Purvis, but for some reason the general manager thought Purvis was golden.

Didn't that figure?

The one weak link in the chain would be the one responsible for his downfall.

Christ, how does one man get so unlucky?

He dressed quickly and was out the door in less than thirty seconds.

By happenstance, Randy lived in the same apartment complex as Tommy Jones, although neither one of them knew the other. Randy could already see smoke down the street as he got in his car.

He arrived in less than a minute, even before the fire department.

CHAPTER FORTY-ONE

At their base, the checkout stations were constructed of metal and were very sturdy. They were made this way because, during the course of a typical day, customers routinely placed very heavy merchandise on wheeled carts and bumped them into the stations; in fact, bumped them into *everything*. Management got tired of repairing cheaply made stations. If there was one part of the operation of the store that could not be interrupted, it was the place where the money was paid.

At the *Emporium*, each station was like a mini-bunker.

Lance was curled up in the U-shaped center of the checkout station on the end. True to its construction, it had performed admirably in protecting Lance from the main part of the explosion and fireball, although he had felt the force of the shock wave. The construction of the checkout stations had actually focused the blast toward the front doors which had borne the brunt of the wave.

The blast itself had been much more powerful than Lance had anticipated. He realized too late that there were many other flammable chemicals on this aisle in addition to the paint thinner cans that he had rigged. The fire he had created had ignited them all.

Lance could feel the heat generated by the fire.

The inferno had made it difficult to breath and his ears were ringing. Lance coughed and then made a yawn-like motion with his jaw as he tried to pop his ears back into duty. Everything sounded like he was in a long tunnel.

And something was wrong. Something he was hearing was not right.

Lance had not intended to blow everything to Hell and back. He had intended only to start a fire in order to set off the automated fire alarm. His hope was that the fire department would be notified and respond to it, preferably in time to save him from being pulverized by Mr. Block-Teeth. During his tour of the *Emporium*, Lance had not seen any manual fire alarms along the walls, although he had been looking. He could not think of a way to summon help other than by actually starting a fire and praying that the detection system would auto-alert the fire department.

He had conceived the idea after being choked.

During his walk to the front of the store after the choke-attack in the back, Lance had passed a huge collection of paint thinners and other flammables on a shelving display that took up a quarter of a wall. He had used the box cutter blade to poke holes in the cans as he walked. He made sure that the holes were small and that he gave each can a double-hole for air intake and ease of drainage.

The tiny holes leaked *slowly*.

In this way, Lance had intended to use the slow leaks as a timer of sorts so he could get to safety before he lit the whole shebang. Once he had hobbled to the checkout station he had discovered that it provided an excellent safety spot to shield him from what he expected to be a very large and fiery explosion. He had almost ignited it while the maniac was still in the back.

Almost.

When Lance had seen the maniac emerge from the back of the store sporting the chainsaw, he had held steady and realized that he could *wait* to light it and trap the crazy bastard as he walked through ground zero unaware. The plan seemed to have worked to perfection, although the blast was more intense and powerful (and produced more heat) than Lance had anticipated.

His hearing was coming back now, and even though he could not see the other man through the smoke, he had a bad feeling. There was still very bad mojo here.

What was out of place?

Sounds.

The chainsaw. Lance heard it. It was *running* and it sounded like it was still coming his way.

Can't be. Simply cannot be.

Lance instinctively grabbed the branch saw that he had used to free the knife from the display case, rolled over on his back, and held the saw in front of him, blade up, just in time to see the man coming at him with the chainsaw still whizzing full throttle in his outstretched hands.

The psychotic fuck was *on fire.*

Jesus! He's on fire! He's coming toward me while he's on fire!

Lance could see that the man had been burned very badly. Was, in fact, *still* burning as the fire concentrated on his face and arms. Black acrid smoke rose from the man's arm as the fire burned the duct tape that held his arm together. Lance saw that the man's eyelids had been burned away, generating the horrific effect of the man's eyes bulging out of their sockets. Lance's gorge rose as he noticed the strip of skin hanging down from the man's right cheek. The fire had burned off the bandage that had held it in place.

The man was coming at Lance, even now.

He had limped to where Lance was lying on the floor and seemed almost to fall forward with the chainsaw, aiming it at Lance's face as he pushed forward. The spinning chain glanced off the teeth of the branch saw Lance held in defense. Sparks flew toward the man's feet as the whirring chain was violently redirected back at the man where it found purchase in the flesh of the right side of his face, sending bloody gore and several teeth streaking along the burning concrete floor.

The chainsaw had opened a huge vertical gash on the side of the man's face, giving his countenance the appearance of having the world's biggest and ghastliest harelip.

The chainsaw went flying from his hands and skidded across the burning floor of the *Emporium*, screeching in outrage as it hit the corner of one of the formidable checkout stations and glanced further down the main aisle, spinning crazily on its side as it went.

Too much.

Lance had finally succumbed to shock, mental now as well as physical, and his only defense–really the only action of which he was capable at the moment–was to simply hold the branch saw in a defensive position.

He could do nothing else.

Now chainsaw-free, Walter simply fell forward toward Lance, across the jagged teeth of the branch saw. In his madness, Walter reached out and carefully placed his hands around Lance's neck.

He began to squeeze.

Lance's mind reeled again from the euphoria that he had felt hiding behind the checkout station and springing his trap, to the unease that he had felt upon hearing the chainsaw after the explosion and fire, to now utter and complete horror as the burning man-corpse choked the life out of him for a second time.

His windpipe clamped shut by the pressure of Walter's hands, Lance could no longer breathe; however, he still could smell the sickening stench as the maniac burned; could actually feel the *heat* clinging to Walter's body as if he had been *cooked* and freshly taken out of the oven.

But the worst, by far, was his face.

It was still *smoking*.

The stench of burnt (*hair? skin?*) was cloying. It seemed to settle around Lance in a light dusting that he could almost taste. The man leaned into the branch saw to gain more leverage so that he could strengthen his grip around Lance's throat. The man made sounds, but they were deep guttural grunts that were not discernable as words.

In the face of this newest assault, Lance could only hold up the saw to keep the maniac from completely collapsing on top of him. Lance could do little more than stare into the face of the man who was choking him.

He saw that the man was grinning.

The wound caused by the chainsaw made the burning man's grin monstrous and impossibly wide. Flecks of bone, flesh and teeth were stuck to the man's chin and continued to drip down the front of his throat.

The burning man's eyes (*what did they see?*) bulged freakishly, looking impossibly large. They were just floating in their sockets now because there was very little flesh to anchor them. The man's body was on fire, and the acrid stench of burning hair and flesh accompanied this hellish vision just six inches away from Lance's own face.

As Walter applied pressure in earnest, Lance's vision began to fade from the lack of oxygen and from the shock of seeing the horror that was on top of him. There was no escape. As before, when the man had locked in the simple choke in the back of the store, black roses bloomed in Lance's vision, the precursor of unconsciousness. Lance was running down the road of resignation, almost thankful now that it would soon be over.

Ain't so bad, not the ideal situation, but it ain't so bad.

Although his lungs were in searing pain, it was his brain that was still active. In Lance's disease-free brain, the primitive module sparked to life again, always eager to assist in these emergencies, and always pissed off that things had to get to this point before it was called upon for advice. This part of Lance's brain was not very good in the idea department, but it was quite adept at making emergency decisions. It was this reptilian part of Lance's brain that, sensing the only route to its continued survival, sent the signal to Lance's hands to get a good strong grip on the branch saw and move it back and forth.

Saw.

It was, after all, what the thing was built to do.

When Walter had fallen onto Lance, the sharp triangular teeth of the branch saw had sunk into the soft flesh of Walter's stomach. When Lance began to move the saw back and forth, the jagged teeth tore through Walter's skin and intestines in only a few short, swift strokes.

It was all Lance could do, but it seemed it might be enough. Lance felt the sickening sensation of resistance as he sensed the saw make its way through the man's mid-section and begin to shear through the vertebrae of his spine.

As the blackness descended upon him, Lance's last thought was of Margie, how good she looked and how it felt to hold her.

The teeth of the saw stuck on something in Walter's mid-section. Lance could no longer move it, could no longer hold the saw out and support the weight of the maniac who was taking his life.

Lance went limp.

He looked up at the man, resigned to his fate and ready to slip away into nothingness. Lance's vision dimmed and he thought he heard thunder from what must have been a thousand miles away.

In the death-grip of Walter Eisenbeis, Lance Davis slipped into unconsciousness.

CHAPTER FORTY-TWO

Tommy had seen some repugnant shit in his life.

As a rookie patrolman he had worked two particularly nasty fatality car accidents. On another occasion, he had been allowed to assist the techs in processing a double-murder scene. And of course, there was always the foul clean-up duty whenever one of the drunks fell asleep on the train tracks (which happened a lot more often than most people would think). But nothing he had seen before was comparable to this.

As he stepped into the *Emporium* through the blast-entrance, Tommy was met with a heat-wall, followed by pungent, foul air and acrid smoke. He took in the odor of burning *(flesh? hair?)* and almost gagged.

Tommy had, of course, been inside the *Emporium* as a shopper many times (on one occasion Purvis Cooper had shown him the exact spot where The Nail Gun Killer had killed the Holmes woman).

As he stepped into the building, even though it was through an unconventional entryway, he was oriented immediately. All the action was taking place at one of the checkout stands to his right. Out of habit, Tommy glanced quickly at all quadrants of the store (better safe than sorry, especially when one works at an insane asylum) before adjusting his body to the right. He then proceeded to walk with caution into smoke, which was always ill-advised, but he had his Glock at the ready in his outstretched hands.

He could hear voices, but could not make them out over the din of some small machine that sounded like a weed trimmer, or possibly a chainsaw.

What the fuck?

Walter was here.

Knew it, fucking knew *it*

Tommy did not know exactly what Walter was doing here. Causing maximum carnage it appeared. Tommy assumed that someone from *Pepe's* had called it in, or perhaps the fire alarm system in the store had auto-alerted the authorities. In any event, Tommy surmised that his window of opportunity would be tight, but doable. The woman outside was still dazed and would hopefully stay out there.

Leaving him alone to take care of *business*.

CHAPTER FORTY-THREE

Randy Philpot arrived at the *Emporium* and his heart sank. It looked like the front doors had been blown out–the glass part anyway–and smoke was billowing out of one side of the security roll-down.

I am double-fucked.

The looky-loos from *Pepe's* had kept a respectable distance, perhaps sensing danger, but a woman stood right next to the opening, on her feet but doubled over like a drunk with the dry-heaves. She seemed to recover and tried to go inside the blast-entrance, but wobbled and hunched forward again.

What in the world is she doing?

As Randy parked as close as he could to the front doors

of the *Emporium*, he was met by a fire truck and could hear more on the way. The firemen were out of the truck quickly and met Randy in the middle.

"Who is that?" asked a fireman, nodding at the woman.

"I don't know," Randy replied, giving a shoulder shrug that said *howthefuckamisupposedtoknow*?

"You the manager?" asked another fireman.

"Yes," Randy replied, not bothering to correct him about the *assistant* part.

Randy looked beyond the fireman who was standing in front of the main entrance where the sliding glass doors should have been. Instead of seeing glass doors marked with giant red letters reading ENTER, Randy saw that, behind the blown out metal security roll-downs, they had been reduced to metal frames standing guard over a sea of shattered glass.

Randy was a creature of habit and, as was his nature, balked at making any big decision, especially under these circumstances where he was clearly out of his element.

Randy was leery of doing it himself since the addition of oxygen from the outside could possibly make the fire worse. Might *vent* it. But hey, he didn't really know and his only expertise on the subject had come from seeing the movie *Backdraft*. The situation was bad enough as it was and he did not want to make things worse. From inside, they could hear what sounded like a

chainsaw?

And then under that sound very loud screams emanating

from just a few feet away from where they stood, judging by the sound of it. He waited for one of the firemen to give some direction regarding entry.

"Open it up!" yelled a fireman.

One of them had tried to enter the *Emporium* through the narrow blast-entrance but his equipment had hung up in the breech and he had been forced to back out. They would have to secure entry via the security doors. Randy turned the key and rolled them up. Despite being expanded outward by the blast, they slid up into place without any problem.

Randy could tell immediately that the fire was not all that large. It appeared to be localized in the paint section. Good, maybe the firefighters could isolate it and keep it from spreading. Might not be so bad after all.

But that God-awful *screaming*.

It set the hairs on the back of Randy's neck on edge, and then rolling out with the screams was the *smell*.

Good God, what was *that?*

The firemen rushed ahead and Randy followed them inside. The woman had finally seemed to get her bearings and she followed after Randy, even though one of the firefighters had told her to get back and stay outside. The open doors ventilated some of the smoke and they gazed upon a scene that they would remember for the rest of their lives.

A man who was burning appeared to be choking another man to death. About ten feet away, a huge black man was holding a handgun pointed at both of them.

The woman pushed Randy out of the way and he stared in amazement as she ran into the fray.

CHAPTER FORTY-FOUR

As Tommy neared the voices, he walked through a smoke-wall which hit a sour note in his tactical mind, but appeared to be necessary if he was gong to capitalize on his good fortune. When he emerged on the other side he was twenty feet from a surreal scene.

His old charge, Walter Eisenbeis, was *on fire* and aiming a chainsaw at a man who was prone behind one of the checkout stations. Walter's head was ablaze and flames licked off both of his arms as he brought the chainsaw down toward the man's *face*.

Tommy saw the whirring chain glance off a metal object the man was holding to defend against the chainsaw and it bounced back directly into Walter's face, digging into his chin. Walter seemed to reflexively fling the chainsaw away and Tommy watched it as it skidded down the aisle, throttle stuck and screaming as it went.

Neither Walter nor the other man–the hapless Lance, Tommy assumed–noticed Tommy.

Tommy trained his Glock on Walter and slowly squeezed the trigger. Walter ducked down suddenly, lunging toward the man on the ground. Tommy released the trigger without firing and re-trained the sights for a better shot, walking forward as he did so. He saw that Walter had lunged forward and was now manually strangling poor old Lance. As he neared the two men, Tommy saw that the metal object in Lance's hands was a tree saw, and that Lance was moving it from side to side, trying to *saw* Walter in half.

Tommy tried to absorb the scene.

He stood there for a few seconds and just watched in amazement. He was morbidly interested to see how it would play out without any outside intervention. Tommy rooted silently for Lance to find the strength to kill Walter right then and there without Tommy having to get directly involved. That would be too good to be true.

C'mon, Lance, saw *that motherfucker.*

Tommy watched this macabre scene as Lance stopped moving the saw back and forth. It appeared to Tommy that Lance had nearly disemboweled Walter, but lacked the strength to finish the job. It was evident that old Lance had petered out and was going to be strangled to death by Walter unless Tommy acted.

Walter leaned in to finish, now without any resistance from Lance. Tommy could see Walter's hands nearly disappear into Lance's neck. The pressure from the squeezing caused Lance's head to look up.

Tommy stepped forward and, at point-blank range, trained the sights on Walter's head. Walter sensed it and looked up with unseeing, scorched eyes as Tommy pulled the trigger twice in rapid succession, then immediately lowered the Glock and fired three times into Walter's torso.

The effect was devastating.

The top of Walter's head disappeared in a spray of blood and gore. He released his grip on Lance's throat as the three body shots punched Walter backward where he tripped and staggered down the aisle, falling finally with a heavy thud on the still-burning concrete.

Lance made no sound, and Tommy wondered if he was still alive.

Tommy wondered if he had waited too long, but that did not diminish the profound sense of relief he felt when he finally put Walter down with his Glock. The chances of Walter being captured alive were now nil. And now so were the chances of old Walter making any sort of scurrilous allegations of misconduct or possible criminal activity against one Thomas Thelonious Jones. Tommy wanted to smile, but suppressed it when he heard sounds behind him.

Problem fucking solved.

Tommy lowered the Glock and turned around. The woman was wide-eyed and walking quickly through the smoke, followed by two firefighters who were yelling at her to fall back and get out of the building and a scrawny fellow who had a stunned look of abject horror on his face. Tommy noticed that the front doors were now wide open and the security roll-ups had been retracted.

"LANCE! OH MY GOD!" screamed the woman.

She took off running and knelt at the side of the prone man by the checkout stand. She screamed for help as she bent down and tended to him. The firefighters were more cautious, eyeballing Tommy.

Tommy immediately understood.

He tucked away the Glock in its holster and hid it from view while he fished in his pocket for his correctional officer badge and raised it up for them to see.

"It's okay, I'm a correctional officer," Tommy said with authority. They nodded and relaxed before running over to assist the woman and to extract the man.

Tommy had learned that in these situations it was always best to say the absolute minimum, if anything at all. One does not want to get locked into a story that one cannot change at a later date, although from the looks of things it appeared that there may have been several witnesses.

Tommy wondered what they thought they saw.

He supposed that he would find out soon enough.

Tommy decided to go outside and let the firemen do their thing. The fire appeared to be contained for the most part, and he sincerely hoped that Lance would be okay, for the sake of the woman if nothing else.

He never even caught her name.

Tommy stepped out of the *Emporium* and waited for the cops to arrive. He saw that the television station was already outside reporting on the incident. Although it had started out as a fire, it was now a potential crime scene as well. Tommy resolved to do what was always the prudent thing to do in these situations.

Keep one's mouth shut and pay attention.

CHAPTER FORTY-FIVE

Outside, one of the EMTs saw Tommy emerge from the building and insisted on treating him for smoke inhalation. Tommy allowed it even though he felt fine. It always seemed to Tommy that first responders, especially the paramedics, needed things to do at these scenes, even if it was not really necessary. Tommy understood this and just decided to go with the flow without complaint.

Besides, he had just shot and killed a man.

A little oxygen might not hurt, especially since the entire area was now a crime scene and he would not be going anywhere soon. In the meantime, he was keen to see if any of the witnesses to the shooting would make any sort of statement.

As he sat in the back of the ambulance, breathing oxygen that he did not need, other EMTs were wheeling Lance out, with his knockout of a wife in tow. Tommy placed the oxygen mask back in its place and exited the back of the ambulance since it looked like they were headed his way. Only one ambulance was at the scene, and Lance was the prime candidate for it.

Tommy stood by as they loaded Lance into the ambulance. He was unconscious and looked to be in pretty bad shape. Tommy did not notice any movement. The woman tried to get inside the ambulance for the ride to the hospital, but an EMT stopped her.

"We need to treat him, ma'am. You can't come in here. Just drive to the hospital and you can meet us there."

"Okay," said the woman softly. She clearly did not want to let go of her husband's hand. Before she did so she held it tightly between her breasts and kissed it before letting go. Although he was not usually moved by such things, Tommy found the gesture touching.

Got a keeper there, Lance.

As she watched the ambulance drive away, the woman crossed her arms, as if she were cold. When it was out of sight, she looked around, as if seeing the outside of the *Emporium* for the first time. It took her a few seconds to notice Tommy, but when she did she ran to him and gave him a big hug and held it there, squeezing him tightly.

She started to cry.

Tommy was genuinely moved.

She took a few moments to regain her composure as she released Tommy from the embrace.

"My name is Marge Davis," she said, wiping away tears from her eyes. "And I want to thank you..." She was too overcome with emotion to finish. Again, she tried to compose herself, wiping the tears away with the sleeves of her shirt. Tommy had no hankie or he would have given one to her.

"And I want to thank you for saving my husband." As she said this, she looked at Tommy with an expression of such gratitude that he could think of nothing to say.

Behind them there was a bustle as the news crew had sniffed out the emotional drama of the exchange. With the predatory instincts of a shark detecting chum in the ocean, the on-air reporter ran to where Tommy and Margie were standing. Tommy recognized the reporter from the local television news, although he noticed that she looked smaller in person than she seemed on television.

The reporter inserted an earpiece and spoke a few clipped words into a handheld microphone. Before going live she leaned over and asked Margie for her name.

Margie had never been interviewed by a reporter in her life and did not know what to do or how to react. She was too emotionally drained at this point to put up must resistance and simply told the impatient woman her name.

When the cameraman was in place and gave a hand signal, the reporter brought a microphone up to her mouth and launched into her piece.

"This is Stephanie Stiles and we are here *LIVE* at the scene of an explosion at *The Builder's Emporium* that has left at least one man dead and several injured. With us is Marge Davis who was inside the building when the explosion happened. Marge can you tell us what happened?"

Stephanie placed the microphone in front of Margie, prompting a response. Margie found her voice.

"It was awful...just the most awful thing you could imagine," said Margie, losing her composure again. As she wiped tears from her eyes, the cameraman zoomed in on her face. She turned suddenly toward Tommy who had tried to slink off into the background and pulled him into the camera shot.

"But this man saved my husband's life," she said tearfully, "Lance was in there, too, and this man, gosh I don't even know his name, he saved him. He saved Lance from that terrible man. Sorry ya'll, but I have to get to the hospital."

And with that, Margie took off running toward her car.

Stephanie Stiles watched her go and, without missing a beat, slid over next to Tommy.

As a rule, Tommy never spoke to the press. Not that the press ever wanted to speak to him, but there were a few occasions when he was on the force where the issue had come up. His old partner had always advised against it. Nothing good can ever come of it, he had said. Tommy agreed. He had seen the way that reporters slanted stories and cut out the important parts of an interview so it would say what they wanted

HARDWARE   301

it to say and not really what the person wanted to say. Worse yet, they always seemed to pick out the most ignorant, backward trailer trash they could find at live scenes and put them on camera to sputter around and look foolish. It was a joke.

But still, there *were* exceptions to every rule, right? And this was *live* after all.

"What is your name, sir?" Stiles asked.

"Thomas Jones."

"Mr. Jones, the woman who just left, Mrs. Davis, stated that you were inside the building and saved her husband's life. Can you tell us what happened in there?"

Tommy screwed on his most serious look and cleared his throat so that his words would be clear.

"This situation was caused by the escaped murderer, Walter Eisenbeis. He was attacking another man in there. I tried to warn him to stop but he continued. I had no choice but to save that innocent man's life. If I had not acted when I did..."

Stiles cut him off.

"Excuse me, Mr. Jones, but are you saying that Walter Eisenbeis, *the Nail Gun Killer*, caused the carnage here tonight and that he is in that building right now, deceased?"

She seemed surprised to hear this bit of news.

"Yes. That is what I am saying," said Tommy without elaborating. That was good enough.

At that moment, a police car and an unmarked detective car pulled up. The uniforms proceeded to set up a perimeter to keep on-lookers back, while the detective, Patrick Gambol, grimaced and made a beeline toward Tommy.

Tommy knew Gambol from way back.

Stiles and her cameraman headed straight for Gambol and immediately peppered him with questions about Walter Eisenbeis, the Nail Gun Killer. Gambol was terse, saying only that the matter was under investigation, before directing one of the uniforms to escort Stiles and the cameraman to the other side of the police tape. The *Emporium* was now officially the site of a crime scene investigation.

Gambol pointed to Tommy.

"Come here," he said without a trace of humor. "You better stick around for a while until we get statements and get this thing straightened out." Gambol lit a cigarette and regarded Tommy as he took a drag.

"Is he really in there?"

"Yeah," Tommy answered.

Gambol exhaled smoke out of his nose as he stared at Tommy.

"Well, then it should be an interesting story."

CHAPTER FORTY-SIX

As it turned out, Tommy had gone down to the station, given a statement and was released. His story was subsequently corroborated by several witnesses, most notably Mrs. Marge Davis, the wife of survivor Lance Davis, as well as Lance himself, as much as he could remember anyway.

Tommy was thereafter officially exonerated in the shooting death of Walter Eisenbeis. The District Attorney ruled the unfortunate event a justifiable homicide.

❦

The Biloxi Sun Herald was the region's largest newspaper. It sent a reporter out to interview Margie and one of the firefighters who had witnessed the shooting (the other had refused to talk about it). The reporter wrote an above-the-fold article that was published about two weeks after the events at *The Builder's Emporium*. The piece included a decent photo of Tommy Jones and read as follows:

The Biloxi Sun Herald
GULFPORT MAN HAILED AS HERO IN NAIL GUN KILLER CASE

by Jefferson Smith

(GULFPORT)–Thomas Jones knows evil. For almost six years, he lived with evil every day at Spring Hill Sanitarium where he supervised the worst of the worst criminally insane patients. There was none worse than the notorious Nail Gun Killer, Walter Eisenbeis, who narrowly avoided the death penalty by being declared legally insane by the Hon. Fife DeBerry. Eisenbeis was responsible for the horrific murder of 27-year-old Amy Holmes, a housewife from Pass Christian. The Holmes murder was one of the most bizarre incidents in Mississippi history. It occurred at a local building supply company in Gulfport where Eisenbeis attacked Holmes with a pneumatic nail gun. She died from her injuries before Eisenbeis could be restrained.

In a bizarre twist, Eisenbeis escaped from

Spring Hill after spending over four years there receiving psychological treatment. He had been scheduled to be transported to Jackson. Officer Jones had come to know Eisenbeis's routines perhaps better than anyone. When Eisenbeis escaped, Jones could not let it go. He thought that there was a good chance that Eisenbeis would return to the scene of his crime. "It was just a hunch," said Jones. His hunch turned out to be eerily accurate. In the early evening hours of the Fourth of July weekend, Jones staked out the original crime scene and just happened to be nearby when an explosion ripped apart the front doors of the business. Inside, Jones found Eisenbeis attacking a customer who had somehow become locked inside the store when it closed. The customer, Lance Davis of Gulfport, was near death from his injuries and most likely would have died at the hands of Eisenbeis had Jones not been on the scene to intercede. Davis does not recall much from the incident, but his wife Marge Davis was also at the scene and described the heroic actions of Jones.

"It was surreal," she said, "that man [Eisenbeis] was choking Lance, just choking the life out him." Marge had to gain her composure before continuing. "Lance looked like a goner and the man just looked so insane. He would not stop, even when Tommy told him to." She wiped tears from her eyes, "[Jones] is a real hero. So is Evan." Evan Brandt was a firefighter at the scene. Brandt had followed Marge into the building and witnessed the awful scene. "[Jones] just shot him when he would not stop attacking Mr. Davis. There was no other course of action to take," said Brandt, who has been with the Department two years.

For his part, Jones remains modest about the tragedy and the part his heroics played in saving Lance Davis. "I just did what anyone else would have done. I'm just glad that I was able to do something for Mr. Davis before it was too late." Jones was cleared by District Attorney Vance Allen who ruled the shooting death of Eisenbeis a justifiable homicide. Today, Jones is back on the job. He does his best to move on and forget that terrible day. Although the events of that day will be with him for a long time, he remains philosophical. "I'm just thankful that I have Jesus in my life. With his help, I know I can get through anything." Jones started his career in law enforcement with the Birmingham Police Department where he was an officer for over twelve years. He has been at Spring Hill for almost six years.

When Tommy read the article he thought it was passable. He marveled at the power of suggestion. He wondered how many times Marge Davis had seen his television interview where he stated that he had warned Walter to stop. The article made it sound like she actually believed that Tommy had said such a thing.

Harmon threw the paper onto his desk with disgust. He stared at Tommy, who had just returned to work after his mandatory administrative leave. Tommy had declined state-sponsored counseling to deal with any issues he might have about shooting and killing Walter. The counseling would have delayed his return. Tommy was eager to get back to work, but before he could return officially he needed Harmon's approval. Harmon was not exactly falling all over himself to give it.

Harmon appeared content to just stare at Tommy. They had played this game many times. Tommy just stood in front of the desk and said nothing. Harmon broke the silence.

"Walter was one of the most well-behaved patients we ever had," Harmon said evenly.

"*That*," he pointed indignantly to the newspaper on his desk, "makes it sound like he walked around here all day eating people."

Tommy said nothing.

It was one of Harmon's usual tactics–making provocative statements in the hopes of eliciting a response.

Of course, Harmon was correct. The irony of it was that Walter had been in the top tier of patients as far as behavior was concerned. He had never given Tommy any problems. For the most part, day in and day out, Walter had never been a problem.

Well, if one doesn't count the whole escaping to commit random murder thingy. There is that.

Tommy thought of saying it, but did not. There was no point. The entire purpose of this little shakedown was so that Harmon could reassert authority over Tommy, and to let Tommy know that Harmon knew that Tommy was dirty, but couldn't prove it.

Harmon had no legal or work-related reason to not allow Tommy back on duty. Tommy had resolved to not give him one, so he stood still and kept quiet.

But the old bastard sure had keen intuition. Tommy had to give it up to him on that count. Just not to his face. Harmon shifted in his chair and smiled, trying charm this time.

"C'mon, Tommy. How the hell did you *really* end up there? Just between us."

"Chance favors the prepared mind, boss."

Tommy had been unable to help himself. He regretted saying it even as the words left his mouth. His old partner had counseled him one time that it was, in fact, perfectly fine to say something that was not nice rather than to say nothing at all. "But," he had said as he had looked out the window of the patrol car, "if you catch yourself about to say something *smartass*, you might want to think it over first."

Tommy mentally kicked himself.

"What the *fuck* are you talking about?" Harmon said, agitated.

"Nothin' boss."

"You gettin' *smart* with me?"

"No, sir."

"Get the fuck outta here."

"Yes, sir."

Tommy turned and walked out the door, eager to get back to work. After all, he was a man with appetites, and there were folks in here who could use a favor or two.

CHAPTER FORTY-SEVEN

The mood inside the law offices of Pamela Denise Chain was subdued. She called the meeting to tie up the loose ends. Dr. Williams did not see the need to personally attend, but she had insisted. Everyone must be on the same page.

She had also instructed him to bring Jeff.

The three of them were quiet in her spacious corner office. Dr. Williams stood facing one of the large bay windows with his hands laced behind his back, staring out into the city as it rained on the light traffic below. Pam sat behind her desk looking at Jeff, who was reading through the statement she had prepared. He sat in one of the chairs facing her desk.

In the hot seat.

The police had requested interviews with both Dr. Williams and Jeff. Jeff had wanted to go immediately to the police station to talk to them, but Dr. Williams had called Pam first to get advice. She had immediately put the kibosh on the interviews and directed them to come to her office first.

When they arrived, she interviewed both Dr. Williams and Jeff about Walter. From what she could gather, Dr. Williams had apparently sent Jeff to visit Walter shortly before "the incident."

During the visit, Jeff had informed Walter of the bad news concerning the brain tumor and the good news concerning the transfer to Jackson. She quizzed Jeff about every detail and had him write out a statement which was then typed by an assistant, formatted, stamped CONFIDENTIAL at the top, and then laser-printed for both Pam and Jeff to review.

Jeff finished reading the document and sat upright, folding the right edge of the sheaf of papers back onto the left edge which created a round tube that he held in both hands.

"Any changes?" Pam asked.

"No," said Jeff, "but why do we have to do it this way? Why can't we just talk to the police and tell them directly?"

Jeff looked uncomfortable.

He was not accustomed to dealing with the police or the criminal justice system. He thought that dodging the request from the police for a formal, in-person interview made it look like he had something to hide; and dealing with the situation through lawyers and typewritten, edited statements just seemed wrong, like he was admitting that he was guilty of something.

Pam had explained to him that it was just a precaution in the event that there was litigation, civil or criminal. She reminded Jeff that Lance Davis could potentially sue Walter's estate, or even *Psychiatry Associates* and Jeff personally if there was any hint that they knew or should have known that Walter might do what he did. Jeff understood the possibility, but was still uneasy.

She tried a different approach.

"Is there anything in the statement that is inaccurate or misleading?" Pam asked.

Jeff looked at her sharply. "No."

"Is there anything else about your meeting with Walter that should be in the report but isn't?"

"No."

"Then what utility is there in meeting with the police?"

Jeff did not respond, but did not look mollified.

"This way we are cooperating fully with the investigation, but leaving no room for any misunderstandings."

Jeff looked over at Dr. Williams who was still quietly looking out the window. Dr. Williams noticed the silence and sensed that Jeff was waiting for his counsel.

"It's the right move, Jeff," he said without pulling his gaze from the window. "You have a long career ahead of you. Do not jeopardize it. You are getting good advice and you need to follow it."

Jeff turned back to Pam.

He frowned as he unfurled the papers in his hand and signed and dated on the bottom line of the last page. He stood, hesitated for a moment, and then tossed the signed statement on her desk.

"None of this was our fault, you know," said Jeff. "I can't believe that anyone would even think that." He said this to no one in particular.

"No one does," said Pam, "but there are unscrupulous people out there always looking to take advantage of a situation. You have to protect yourself."

Jeff looked at Dr. Williams who made no comment.

"I'm going to wait outside," said Jeff. He walked out of the office, leaving the door to close slowly on an automatic arm mounted at the top. When the door was fully closed, Pam broke the uncomfortable silence.

"Do you remember when you were that naive, David?

"We all were at one time, Pam."

"Debatable."

Dr. Williams heard the whir of two high-end air purifiers and turned around to see Pam light a cigarette in the non-smoking building.

"I thought you quit."

"Your methods were inadequate."

"As I recall, that was not the only thing about me that you found inadequate."

She let the comment pass and took a long drag on her cigarette.

Dr. Williams resumed his posture at the window. He regretted not handling the matter himself and getting Jeff entangled in a situation like this. The kid did not deserve it. Pam had a way of doing things. If he had gone to visit Walter rather than Jeff, the entire situation would have been streamlined because Dr. Williams found it easy to take direction from Pam. The young man simply asked too many questions.

Even with the expensive air purifiers humming on high, Dr. Williams could smell the aroma of Turkish cigarette smoke. He had no idea where she got them.

"What is the exposure to the estate?" he said.

"Minimal. New York says the trusts are ironclad. Walter was cut out years ago. No rights to the corpus, just subsistence through disbursements that expired upon his death. Including legal and medical expenses, of course."

"New York?"

Pam leaned back in her chair and crossed her legs.

"If you have a trust valued at three hundred dollars, you go to Jackson," she blew a plume of smoke into the air and then looked at Dr. Williams, "if you have one valued at three hundred million you go to New York."

Dr. Williams nodded.

"Has Davis made overtures?"

"None so far. Probably has not even talked to a lawyer, but chances are decent that one will talk to him. He has two years to file suit. We sit and wait it out. We don't do anything *stupid.*"

"What about Jeff? Hell, what about *me*?"

"Relax," she said as she leaned back in her chair. "His statement is bulletproof. No prior knowledge of anything and nothing reasonably foreseeable. Just make sure that you keep him on the reservation. If anyone should be puckering it's Spring Hill for allowing the escape, but state law is with them. It's formidable."

Pam leaned forward and set the cigarette in an ashtray on her desk.

"What was Walter's score on that test?" she asked.

"The Hare?"

"Yes."

Pam was referring to the revised Psychopathy Checklist or PCL-R. It was a diagnostic instrument developed by Dr. Robert Hare, a Canadian psychologist.

Its purpose was to identify psychopaths.

"The last time I administered it he scored a thirty-nine point seven."

"What is the max?"

"Forty. A person scoring thirty or above is considered to be a psychopath. Walter excelled."

Pam whistled, lighting up another cigarette and leaning back in her chair.

Dr. Williams turned and walked to her desk, stopping at a chair to pick up his suit coat.

"Did you know that I gave Walter an IQ test about three years ago? I administered it myself. He scored a 169. That was about the time when he first arrived at Spring Hill. The test was legit, Pam. I saw him take it. Far less than point zero zero one percent of the world's population could score that high."

"Impressive," said Pam. "I should probably come over some time so you can test me."

"IQ or Hare?"

"Which do you prefer?"

Dr. Williams put on his coat and opened the door.

"I'm afraid that you might score higher than Walter on both."

"Take care, David."

"You, too, Pam."

CHAPTER FORTY-EIGHT

The body of Walter Samuel Eisenbeis was interred at Calvary Eternal cemetery in Jackson, Mississippi. He was buried next to his mother.

CHAPTER FORTY-NINE

Lance was hospitalized for nearly a week after his ordeal at the *Emporium*. His primary physical infirmities were the injury to his right ankle, severe dehydration, infection caused by the cuts on his body, a bruised larynx, and exhaustion. He had to have stitches in various places on both hands, his right calf, and his scalp.

When Walter had used the hatchet to chop Lance's right ankle, it had actually severed his Achilles tendon. Amputation was not necessary, but it remained to be seen whether Lance would ever regain full use of that foot. He left the hospital in a wheelchair, but had since been able to hobble around on crutches, although he had great difficulty doing so.

One month after the incident, Chet (Lance's inimitable nephew) was over at the house helping Margie move some heavy things around. Chet had been over a lot lately. Lance suspected that things were not going so good with Charlie, Chet's father.

Lance reflected on his childhood, as he had been reflecting on a lot of things lately. Charlie had been a great brother to Lance. Still was. But Lance could see now that Charlie had not been a great son to their parents, and there was no denying the fact that Charlie was still trying to find his way to be a good father to Chet. Charlie had been awarded custody of Chet after the divorce, but things had never been the same after the family had split, as they never are.

Since his ordeal, Lance had tried to think of things he could do to help Chet find his way. In the end, he supposed that just being around was the best he could do. Being around was good enough most of the time and, before long, Lance discovered that he had needed some help, too.

Having Chet around was a comfort.

Lance had told everyone that he could not remember much of what happened to him at the *Emporium* but, in truth, he remembered almost everything. It had come back to him in memory-chunks since his release from the hospital. He thought that being back home had something to do with it. He tried to forget it just as fast as he had remembered it. He had told no one about it.

Not even Margie.

It was only much later that he had found out that she had witnessed the end of his ordeal; that she had seen him being choked nearly to death inside the store. Lance found it unbearable that Margie had to see something like that. In a way that he could feel but could not articulate, knowing that she had been exposed to such a horrific scene was in some ways worse than having experienced it himself.

He felt tremendous guilt over this because she had come for him. Although his rational mind recognized that the ordeal was not his fault, his clenched jaw and grinding teeth carried a different message. It *was* his fault. Margie was there because she was looking for him. She had to see that horror because he was involved in it.

And why was he involved in it? How did that happen?

He had left her alone and went out to *Cat Calls* with Frank and Carl, not thinking about her a single time while he was there. But when he hadn't come back, she had gone out looking for him, unaware that she was going to be dragged into a surreal nightmare.

And she had known that he was in there. Somehow she had known. If that guard, Jones, hadn't been there, Lance knew that she would have run to him and faced that lunatic by herself.

To save him.

Such selflessness was love in its purest form. Had he not seen it before? How had he not appreciated her in this way during their years of marriage? And then, deeper into the recesses of his mind: would he have done the same for her?

That question was the killer. He had thus far avoided answering it, afraid of what the honest answer would be and what it might reveal about himself.

This was the train of thought in Lance's head each time he tried to wrap his mind around his ordeal. It always ended up there, with him imagining Margie inside the *Emporium* fighting that lunatic in order to save him (and herself most likely) while he was passed out and useless.

She *would* have done that; had in fact *tried* to do it, but was spared a confrontation with the madman by nothing more profound than dumb luck. Lance did not think he could have gone on living if it had played out that way. In fact, he was sure of it. Since it had not played out that way, he felt obliged to keep going. But making it up to Margie was going to take some big changes, or perhaps lots of little changes.

That was the way he thought of it, even though everyone said that it was not his fault. But who else was there to blame? Lance did not particularly blame the lunatic, much like he would not blame a rabid dog that tried to bite him. The lunatic was not the one with the hangover. And who was it that had not been paying attention in the store when it closed? Who was it that shit on his own hand and broke his cell phone? Who was it that almost got strangled to death and could do nothing about it?

Lance had not been prepared for the guilt. Had in fact been surprised when it came. The mental fatigue it caused was in many ways worse than his physical injuries.

Am I the same man I was before this ordeal? Could I

be? If I've changed, does Margie sense it? What does she think? Is all of it in my head?

Lance was deep in thought on these issues as he reclined in his easy chair. He had just taken two Percocet and was extremely relaxed, although not yet sleepy. It was at these times when his mind drifted to what had happened, and to what could have been.

Lance's concentration was interrupted when Chet came into the den.

Margie was still making noises in the kitchen.

Chet regarded Lance, who was blinking and stretching in the recliner. Chet sat down on the couch opposite Lance and fiddled around, looking at the floor. Looking *nervous*. Lance was still and regarded his nephew. He realized that he had not given any thought to how his experience at the *Emporium* might have affected Chet. As he felt the Percoset grip his system, Lance made a mental note to think it through later, when he was not doped up on painkillers.

On the couch, Chet was still fidgeting. Lance couldn't take it anymore.

"What?" Lance asked, breaking the uncomfortable tension in the room. Chet looked up and met Lance's eyes.

"What was it like?" asked Chet. "What happened in there?"

Lance considered the questions. The boy was curious, which was natural enough. The *Emporium* ordeal was certainly something that stoked curiosity. As a result of the media attention it seemed that the entire Gulf Coast wanted the details. Now someone close to him had asked him directly. Lance did not seriously consider answering. For now, at least, those details were for Lance, and him alone. He might choose to open that dark door someday. But not today.

Maybe not ever.

"You don't want to know," replied Lance, looking away and not offering anything else.

Chet looked as if he would press it, but said nothing. He stood up and walked over to Lance, not sure what to do and clearly uncomfortable. He put his hands in the pockets of his jeans to keep them from roaming around and said simply, "I'm going to take off. I'll see you later."

He turned around to leave.

Lance called, "Hey, Chet."

Chet stopped and turned around, waiting for Lance to speak.

"Thanks for helping Margie out." Lance took a breath. "Thanks for helping *me* out."

It came out with a little bit more emotion than Lance had intended, and he saw that Chet was still uncomfortable, not sure of what to say.

Chet just nodded. Then he walked toward the door and let himself out. Lance listened to the sound of Chet's car engine come to life and then fade as he drove away.

Margie came into the room with sweet tea and placed the glass on the end table. She sat down on the couch and turned on the television. They did not watch much television, but it was Thursday night and her favorites were in the line-up. Lance looked at her and cleared his throat. He just had a strong urge to say it before he drifted off to sleep.

"I *love* you, Margie."

Margie looked at him and smiled.

"I love you, too."

THE END

ACKNOWLEDGMENTS

Preparing a novel for the eyes of the world takes a lot of work, much more than I had anticipated. I just figured that all I would have to do is write the damn thing. But once that was done, I discovered that there was much more work to be had.

I'd like to thank Patty Hankins and Leya Booth for taking out the mushy parts and making it presentable.

Also, a special thanks to Leslie the Pooh Bear for designing the greatest book cover in the world; to Jamie for his keen insights and editing skills; and to Bubba for giving it a critical review. Finally, a special thanks to Alisa for her love and support. Always.

Finally, the creepy blood droplets on the back cover were provided by Simon Howden at freedigitalphotos.net.

NOTE: A note on George Carlin. Lance took Margie out to the *Beau* for their anniversary, during which they caught Carlin's show. Between the creation of this book and the editing process, Mr. Carlin passed away. I had considered changing the scene to include a living comedian, but upon consideration I decided to leave George in as an homage to a man who was a critical thinker and funny as hell.

ABOUT THE AUTHOR

James Hankins lives and writes in Oklahoma City. HARDWARE is his first novel. He is working on other writing projects, including a horror-themed short story collection, and a second novel about a man who cheats on his wife and the horrible things that happen to him. James can be contacted at:

www.jameslhankins.com

www.ingramcontent.com/pod-product-compliance
Lightning Source LLC
Chambersburg PA
CBHW070216260626
47160CB00002B/569